Dead or a Lie

A Henry Walsh Mystery

Gregory Payette

8 Flags Publishing, Inc.

Copyright © 2024 by Gregory Payette

8 Flags Publishing, Inc.

Print ISBN: 979-8-9876219-7-4

Ebook ISBN: 979-8-9876219-6-7

All rights reserved.

This book is licensed for your personal enjoyment only. All rights reserved. This is a work of fiction. All characters and events portrayed in this book are fictional, and any resemblance to real people or incidents is purely coincidental. This book, or parts thereof, may not be reproduced in any form without permission in writing from the publisher or author, except as permitted by U.S. copyright law.

For Julia

Acknowledgements

I don't always include acknowledgements, but it's time I do. This is the tenth book in the Henry Walsh series. Eleventh, with the prequel. Therefore, more than one thank you is more than overdue. My books wouldn't exist without the people around me who lend more than just a hand.

Of course, I'll thank my wife, Megan, for your support, for listening to my ideas (even the bad ones) and reading my books when they're not quite there yet. Thank you to my kids, Julia and James, for inspiring me with your intelligence and good hearts. (They are both now old enough to give me advice.) To my cousin, John, for listening to me about my books and asking so many questions, the way Uncle Richard used to. To Jen and Denise, for your feedback. To my mom, for always looking forward to my next book. Leaving me messages in the early days, and how excited you were that I wrote a good book, gave me the juice to keep going.

I also want to thank the CM police department, for the insight and education I received, giving me a better understanding of police work. Thank you to Dean Wesley Smith, for teaching me how to write into the dark and have fun.

And finally, thank you to Paula and Terry, my editor and proofreader. My books wouldn't be what they are without you.

There are others I know I'm forgetting.

Of course, thank you to my readers, for enjoying my stories and making it possible for me to keep doing what I love. These books are for you.

Books by Gregory Payette

For the full catalog of books,
please visit GregoryPayette.com

HENRY WALSH MYSTERIES
Dead at Third
The Last Ride
The Crystal Pelican
The Night the Music Died
Dead Men Don't Smile
Dead in the Creek
Dropped Dead
Dead Luck
A Shot in the Dark
Dead or a Lie

JOE SHELDON SERIES
Play It Cool
Play It Again
Play It Down

U.S. MARSHAL CHARLIE HARLOW
Shake the Trees
Trackdown

JAKE HORN MYSTERIES
Murder at Morrissey Motel
Body on the Beach

Sign up for the newsletter on my website:

GregoryPayette.com

Once or twice a month I'll send you updates and news. Plus, you'll be the first to hear about new releases with special prices. If you'd like to receive the Henry Walsh prequel (for free) use the sign-up form here:

https://www.gregorypayette.com/pages/freecrossroad

Chapter 1

One of the things I liked about living on a boat was the yard work it required. It was a good life while it lasted, being on that boat. But I left it behind, trading my old life on the water for one in suburbia, coincidentally in the same house where I was raised.

I'd quickly become just like every other homeowner in the neighborhood, taking out the trash every Tuesday morning, or pushing a mower in the hot sun at least once a week.

Even if I hadn't lived on a boat for all those years, lawn up-keep was never something I'd put high on my list of priorities. I never understood the obsession with having a perfect lawn.

There was a guy who lived down the street, fifth house on the right, who seemed to be out working on his lawn just about every day. Any time I'd drive by, he'd be out there, mowing or trimming. or sometimes down on his hands and knees as if studying each blade to ensure it was of the finest quality in the neighborhood. The thing I found funny was he had a wife and kids, but I felt if he had to make a choice between spending time with them or the lawn? He'd take the lawn.

And don't get me started on the leaf blowers...

It'd been a few months since Alex and I officially moved into the house together. As I'd mentioned, it was the house I grew up in, which honestly felt more than just a little strange once the deal was done. I wouldn't say I regretted the move; it seemed to make sense when we first approached the owners who bought it from my parents. And it didn't hurt that it'd been completely remodeled, which meant it wasn't like I was walking into my old bedroom where I slept for eighteen years, or the same dining room where we'd eaten hundreds of meals as a family.

It would take some getting used to.

But, the truth was, waking up next to Alex every morning was far from a bad life.

I walked behind the mower, pushing it from one end of the lawn to the other. It was a monotonous process I dreaded. My mind wandered. But I felt I needed to do my share around the house.

I won't lie; Alex put up a good chunk of her own money to buy the house. Most of it came from the proceeds she got after selling her house in Arlington before she took a detective job in North Carolina.

It's not as if I didn't contribute at all. But I wasn't exactly rolling in dough. If someone wanted to become rich, getting into the PI business wasn't the best path.

Of course, I knew I could take Walsh Investigations to another level as a business, if I wanted to. But the next level would mean hiring employees. I wasn't sure that was something I'd be up for.

I'd managed a small staff when I was the security director for the Jacksonville Sharks baseball team, along with Alex who, at the time, was technically my assistant. But half of my time was spent as a babysitter for the rest of the staff—Alex aside—and I knew it wasn't my thing.

I had a hard enough time taking care of myself.

The good news was, Alex was back in my life, and we made a pretty good team, in more ways than one.

We were a soon-to-be-married couple living in a nice house in Fernandina Beach, Florida, no more than a couple of miles from the ocean.

Alex laughed when I told her I'd mow the lawn myself. She felt my time could be put to better use, and wanted to hire a professional. But I insisted we didn't need to spend more money. Not until Walsh Investigations was more profitable.

I wasn't sure that would ever happen.

I wiped the sweat from my forehead with the back of my arm, looking around at the half-cut lawn. I wanted to quit, even though the lawn wasn't huge. It still took me forever.

Back and forth.

I was tempted to do something to the mower, so when Alex got home and saw the half-mowed lawn I could tell her the thing broke.

That's a trick I used as a kid a couple of times, so I could head to the beach with my friends when I was supposed to be mowing the grass.

But my dad was a pretty laid-back guy. And half the time I'd get home from my summertime excursion and the lawn would be cut.

Dad wouldn't say a word about it.

That's just how he was.

I still remember the day I knocked a baseball through the front picture window, crying because I was sure I'd be in trouble. But Dad got home from work, stepped out of his car, and the first thing he asked me was if it was fair or foul.

Alex pulled in the driveway in her yellow Jeep. I turned off the mower and heard Raz barking from inside the house.

He was excited. His favorite person was home.

Alex climbed down from her Jeep and walked around to the passenger side. She reached in for two bags of groceries and carried one in each arm up the walkway to the house, keys dangling from her fingers.

"You want some help?" I said, trying to take the bags from her before she answered.

She pulled them back from me. "You're all sweaty." She sniffed and crinkled her nose before continuing to the house. She glanced at the unfinished lawn. "Can't we just hire someone?"

I said, "Yeah, if you want to spend a hundred bucks a week we can."

Alex headed up the brick steps and didn't respond, trying to reach for the doorknob while balancing one of the bags on her raised thigh.

I stepped past her, opened the door, and took both bags from her grasp before she could object.

The cool, air-conditioned air felt good inside. Raz was seated on the hardwood, tail wagging, eyes directed up to Alex waiting for her to pet him. She crouched down and rubbed his face, the two acting like they hadn't seen each other in weeks.

I placed the bags on the counter in the kitchen and turned as Alex walked through the doorway. I said, "Maybe we should go out, get something to eat."

Alex laughed. "Go finish the lawn. I'll make lunch."

· · · • · • • • · · ·

Alex had a drink in her hand when I walked back into the house after finally finishing the lawn. She was standing over her laptop on the counter, and turned to me. "Your lawn mowing days are over. I just scheduled a guy to come out, starting next week. Now you can focus on the business, instead of procrastinating."

"Procrastinating? You really think I'm..." I held up my phone. "It's been three weeks since this phone's rung. And I'm pretty sure the last call was someone with the wrong number."

I placed the phone on the table, but as soon as I did it vibrated. I picked it up and saw my friend Billy Wu's face on the screen.

I answered as if it was the old days, when you didn't know who was calling. "Hello?"

"Henry?" he said. "Where are you?"

"Where *am* I?" I said, sensing something was wrong. Usually when someone starts a call with a question and not a greeting, there's a good chance something's wrong.

"I'm at the house," I said. "What's wrong?"

"You need to get over here," he said.

"Over *where*?"

"The restaurant." Billy's voice got somewhat hushed. "There's someone here looking for you."

"Does this person have a name?"

Billy paused on the other end before answering, his voice a whisper. "Brock."

I glanced at Alex standing in front of the fridge with the door open, her back to me. I turned and went outside where I could have some privacy.

The smell of the fresh-cut grass hit me as soon as I stepped out.

"Brock?" I said. "Brock Mason?"

"I don't know. I've never seen him before. But he's had a few. I'm about to cut him off."

I hadn't heard the name Brock Mason in at least ten, maybe even fifteen years.

"He say what he wants?"

"I didn't ask. He said he'd gone upstairs to your office, then came down asking for you. I thought I'd check with you first, before I gave him your number."

"I appreciate that," I said.

Billy paused on the other end. "If I had to guess, he's in some kind of trouble."

"Based on what?" I said, even though Billy was as perceptive as anyone I'd ever met, and usually could successfully read just about any situation.

"He asked how long you've been a PI, but I didn't give him any details. I didn't tell him we were friends or anything either, just that you rent the office space from me."

Man, if there was an old friend I didn't think I needed to see again, it was Brock Mason.

Back after I'd left Rhode Island, wandering around Florida trying to find my new path, I ended up hitting the sauce pretty hard and hanging around with some real losers. Not that they were all bad people, but I couldn't think of a different way to describe them. I'm sure plenty of people described me the same way at the time.

I know *I* did.

But, if, at the time, I wanted to find trouble, I was hanging with the right crowd to get me there. That crowd included Brock Mason.

"You want me to give him your number?" Billy said.

I had to think about it. It wasn't like he couldn't find it on his own. But, Brock wasn't exactly what you'd consider resourceful. It wouldn't have surprised me if he still didn't own a cell phone, or know how to use a computer. And not just because he was older than me by a few years. He didn't like authority. Or the government. He certainly didn't trust technology.

But that was a long time ago. And, thinking back, maybe his beliefs weren't as crazy as they seemed at the time.

"Tell him to stay where he is," I said, looking at my watch. Billy's Place, and my office upstairs from it, wasn't exactly nearby. Since we'd moved out to Fernandina Beach, the drive was close to forty minutes. "I'll be there as soon as I can."

Chapter 2

I KNEW IT WAS foolish, but on the ride to Billy's Place I wasn't exactly straight with Alex about what Brock Mason was really all about. All I told her was that I knew him from the past.

I left it at that.

But Alex might've started thinking about it when we walked into the restaurant and Brock jumped from the bar when he saw me. He wrapped me up in a bear hug so tight I could barely breathe, then went as far as slapping a kiss on my cheek, leaving a stain of wet saliva and booze on my face.

I could smell the whiskey on his breath, on top of whatever cheap cologne I imagined him buying from the counter at 7-Eleven.

Brock had aged, his longish hair more gray than blond now. He was still a good-looking man, with a few extra pounds on him since the last time I saw him.

I glanced back at Alex watching us, an unsure smile on her face.

"So, how you been, buddy?" he said, looking me over. "You look good. Aged a bit, but..."

It was clear Brock had already had a few drinks, with the way he had those red, puffy eyes and the familiar sleepy look he'd get after putting back a few.

I introduced Alex and Brock to each other, and the way he looked her over, I thought she was going to reach out and crack him, if I didn't do it first.

"She's my fiancée," I said, making it clear with the tone in my voice he'd need to show some respect.

"Your fiancée?" He held his gaze on me, with a slight grin as if he didn't believe it, then reached for a glass from the bar and raised it. "Congratulations," he said, throwing his head back and finishing whatever was in the glass. "Looks like you hit the jackpot." He turned and waved for the bartender, Chloe, watching us from behind the bar. Brock held up his empty glass. "Can we get a round over here, sweetheart?"

Chloe gave me a look, knowing I hadn't had a drink in almost a year, and I wasn't about to start just because Brock Mason was in town.

I said to Brock, "Thanks, but not right now."

"You don't want a drink?" He snorted out a laugh, shaking his head, looking at Alex with his thumb pointed my way. "Hank? Turning down a drink? I guess you got that leash nice and tight on him there, honey?"

Alex didn't respond, only forming a smirk I could tell she wanted to hold back, but couldn't. She had to've been wondering who this guy was, and why I didn't give her more of a heads-up on the ride over.

When Brock and I hung out, it was at a low point of my life. There were some dark times after I lost or—on paper—*resigned* from my job with the Rhode Island State Police. I wasn't even much of a drinker when I was younger. But when I moved back to Florida alone, out of work with nowhere else to go, I met a friend named Jack Daniels.

And we played hard.

That's when I met Brock Mason. I'm not even sure how or where. It was a bar. That's the only part I remember.

Brock said, "So, shall we sit?" He looked around at the empty tables. "This place always this dead?"

"It's the middle of the day," I said, coming off a little defensive, considering the restaurant was owned by my good friend.

Billy was a *real* friend. Always there for me when I needed one. Along with Alex, there weren't many other people in life I'd depended on as much as them.

But Brock? It was hard to say what kind of friend he was, or if I'd even consider him one at all. He was more of a drinking buddy, back in the day. Seeing him again brought back memories, as fuzzy as they were, I'd hoped to leave in the past.

Brock grabbed the drink Chloe had put on the bar for him, took a sip and walked past the empty stools to a table on the other side of the bar, away from everything else, where the lighting was dim. "Let's sit down," he said, walking ahead of me and Alex.

I said, "So, Brock. Can I ask what this is all about?"

He stopped with that dumb look on his face, like I was the one who'd asked a stupid question. He threw his arm around my shoulder. "Can't I just come out to Jax to see an old buddy?"

I rolled my eyes.

I was no fool.

Alex sat first and took the stool nearest the wall, and before I could sit, Brock nudged me out of the way and sat on the stool next to her.

She had a look on her face like she wasn't sure if she should laugh or get up and move. But she stayed where she was, and I sat across from them.

Brock sipped his drink and slapped the glass down on the table. "You sure you don't want a drink?" he said. "Come on, Hank. For old time's sake, huh?"

I thought about how nobody else ever called me Hank. And he knew I didn't like it. But the one time I told him not to call me that, all it did was make him say it more, from that point forward.

Alex looked at me and smiled when he said it.

"Maybe later," I said, knowing he'd have a field day if I told him I'd given up the drinking.

Chloe, not only the bartender, but also the manager of Billy's Place, came around from behind the bar and asked me and Alex if we wanted anything.

We ordered iced tea, and when Chloe carried them to the table, she put a glass of water in front of Brock. It wasn't as if water would sober him up, but she seemed to be hinting he'd had enough.

Brock looked up at her, like he was confused about what it was. But he took a sip and seemed satisfied with the hydration. "Thanks, sweetheart."

Chloe put on her best smile, clearly forced. "You're welcome." I could tell by the look on her face as she turned to walk away, she'd had enough of Brock.

Alex said, "So, Brock, Henry tells me you used to live around here?"

He nodded. "I'm in Miami now. But who knows what's next. It used to be a cheap place to live and have a good time, but those days are long gone."

"You're not coming back up here, are you?" I said.

"You make it sound like I'm not welcome," Brock said, a crooked grin on his face.

"Didn't intend it that way. Just asking," I said.

Brock looked at his curled fingers, bit a nail and spit a piece of it on the floor.

I watched Alex's eyes widen in disgust.

"I'm thinking maybe I'll take off for a while," Brock said. "I don't know. Maybe hit the West Coast. Even thought about New England once or twice, but I don't think I'd like the cold. Just got some business I gotta take care of down there, then we'll see what's next."

"What kind of business?" I said.

Brock shrugged, pushing his water aside. He grabbed the glass with the booze in it, looking at me over the rim as he raised it to his lips. He said, "Just business."

He hadn't said much of anything about why he was there, and I couldn't help but wonder if maybe it was because of Alex.

Brock said, "So, how long've you two lovebirds been together?"

Neither one of us answered.

"Brock," I said, "Why don't you just tell me what you're doing here?"

His goofy smile dropped from his face and he looked into his glass. "I need to find someone," he said. "And I ain't having much luck by myself. I thought maybe, you know, I'd see if I could get some help."

"Some help?" I said. "I assume you mean, help from me?"

Brock smiled, but didn't say anything else.

I gave Alex a quick glance, and could tell by the look on her face she wasn't interested in this particular prospective client.

"What's it about?" she said.

I was surprised she'd asked.

"What's it about?" Brock said. He sipped what was left in his glass and held the ice cube in his mouth, chewing it for a couple of moments without a response.

"Just someone I'm looking for. A friend."

"A friend?" I said. "She's missing?"

Brock seemed to hesitate, then nodded. He didn't get into any specifics.

"Why not call the cops?" I said. "That's what you do, when someone is missing."

Brock shook his head. "Nah, it's not like that."

"Like what?" Alex said.

He cleared his throat, turning the empty glass in his big hand, eyes down. He said to Alex, "You mind if me and Hank here have a talk? Nothing personal, but..."

"Anything you need to say to me, you can say to Alex," I said.

But Alex gave me a look, like she felt like she was better off not being a part of the conversation. She stood up from the table. "I'll be upstairs." She continued out the door without another word.

"I didn't mean to offend her," Brock said.

I took a deep breath and nodded. "It's fine,' I said. "Just tell me what's up."

Brock shifted in her seat, leaning closer to me over the table. "I heard you were some kind of private investigator, but wasn't sure you'd—"

"Let's cut the small talk," I said. "If you didn't call the cops about this so-called friend of yours, then I'm going to assume this isn't some kind of life-or-death situation. What is she, just another girlfriend trying to get away from you?"

Brock laughed. "Something like that," he said. His expression turned serious. "I gotta find her. What more do you need to know?"

"Plenty," I said. "I'm not going to jump into something like this, just because you show up here asking. If you can't give me the details, then—"

"Her name's Jillian. Jillian Rogers."

"She lives her in Jax?" I said.

"Well, not exactly. But I hear she's up here."

"You hear?" I said. "What's that mean? *You hear.*"

"She's someone I... You're right about the girlfriend part. I mean, not exactly, but..."

I was starting to lose patience. "Jesus, Brock. Will you just tell me what the deal is? If you want my help, you're going to have to be straight with me. I know that's not always easy for you, but that's the way it's going to be."

"Whoa," he said. "What's that supposed to mean? I'm not the same old Brock, you know. People can change."

I said, "If you think you're going to walk in here and try to get me wrapped up in one of your schemes..."

"There's no scheme, Hank. I'm serious. She's just someone I gotta find. The truth is, she might not even be up here anymore. But if you can at least help me figure that part out, then I'm good. I'll get out of here. She could be back in Miami, for all I know."

"Is that where she's from?" I said.

Again, he nodded.

By that point I was tempted to get up and walk away.

I said, "If you think I'm going to Miami…"

Brock waved his hand. "No, no. I'm not asking you to. But I don't know where she is. If I did, I wouldn't be here asking for your help. And, listen, Hank. I'm not asking for any favors. Whatever your rate. I'm good for it. You know that."

I knew what it meant when someone said they were good for something. It usually meant they weren't, and I'd be lucky if I ever got whatever it was they were good for.

That was Brock. The only thing he was good for was empty promises.

"Here's the deal," I said, leaning forward with my elbows on the table. "I'm not doing a thing without the details. If you can't be straight with me, then I'm sorry. I can't help."

"You don't trust me?" he said.

I almost laughed, shaking my head. "No."

Brock didn't appear to like my answer.

"All I'm asking is for her location," he said. "I'm sure you have ways of finding someone, right? You don't have to do anything else."

"You make it sound easy," I said. "You think I'm just going to walk up to my office, get on the computer and find the answer?"

Brock shrugged. "I don't know. Why not?"

"I'm sorry," I said. "But you don't tell me the reason you're looking for this woman, I'm not going to be able to help you. It's just how things have to work. Okay?"

He waited, his gaze somewhere else now, across the restaurant.

After a moment he looked back at me, leaning forward, voice hushed. "She could be in some kind of trouble."

"What kind of trouble?" I said.

Brock remained silent. "Come on, Hank. The details aren't going to make a difference, are they?"

With that, I was done.

I stood up from the table. "I think I understand why you won't call the cops. You're involved in something shady. What a surprise. And you think I'm going to get involved in whatever it is you've got yourself wrapped up in?" I shook my head and turned from the table. "Great seeing you, Brock."

"Hank, wait," he said, following after me.

I tossed a couple of bills on the bar for Chloe as I walked by, enough to hopefully cover whatever Brock had put back and the two iced teas Alex and I didn't touch. I said to her, "Tell Billy I'll be upstairs."

Chloe was wiping out a glass, nodding with a serious look on her face. She knew something was off.

Brock followed me outside, the hot sun blasting me in the face as we stepped onto the slate landing outside the front door. I slipped my sunglasses on and turned to him standing behind me. "I'm sorry," I said.

But he grabbed me by the arm before I started to walk away, squeezing it more than I liked.

I yanked free from his grasp. "Don't," I said. "I'm serious."

Brock put both hands up and took a step back. "I'm sorry," he said.

I had played Brock's games before. There was a reason we'd lost touch. It wasn't by accident.

"You're worried about her? Then call the police," I said, walking away from him. I continued around the building and stopped before I got the exterior stairs to the second level. I expected he would've followed. But he didn't.

I was at the top of the stairs when I heard a loud engine roar, then rev-up like some kind of muscle car on the racetrack. Sure enough, a few seconds later a black Dodge Charger, one of those newer models, squealed its tires and took off across the parking lot.

My first thought was Brock had been drinking, and I didn't like the idea he'd gotten behind the wheel. On the other hand, I wasn't sure if it was even him, the way the windows were tinted, making it hard to see inside.

I watched the Charger skid out of the lot and onto Virginia Street, the car's rear end fishtailing as the engine growled. The vehicle took off like a rocket, heading northeast toward Buffalo Avenue.

I walked back down the stairs and to the front of the building. Looking around, it appeared Brock was gone.

Chapter 3

ALEX WAS AT HER desk when I walked into the office, looking up at me from her laptop as I closed the door. She said, "How come you left out the part about your friend being an ex-con?"

"An ex-con?" I said, acting like I was surprised.

She said, "Are you going to tell me you didn't know he did three years in Union Correctional?"

I shook my head. "I would have told you if I did," I said. "What'd he do?"

She held her gaze for a moment, eyes narrowed as if she didn't believe me, then looked back at the screen. "He was charged with wire fraud, something about a nonprofit down in Miami that was supposed to help ex-prisoners find work after their release. It doesn't appear it was legit."

"Is he the only one convicted?" I said.

"The organization's CFO, a man named Vincent Giotti, was sentenced to seven years. Brock got five. He's been out two years."

I walked over and stood behind Alex in her chair, my eyes on the computer screen. "What made you do this?" I said.

"Do what?"

"Look up Brock's background?"

She gave a slight shrug. "I figured if you're going to help an old friend, I should at least know what we're getting into."

"He's just someone from my past," I said. "From days I'd just as soon forget."

She turned in her chair, eyes on me. "So you don't want to know what else I found?"

I nodded, waiting.

Alex picked up a pad from the desk and leaned back in her chair, looking over whatever she'd written on the top sheet. "It looks like he was working for this place, Canzano Waste Management, back in Miami when he was convicted."

I said, "What about it?"

"The company's owned by this guy from New York. His name's Ray Canzano."

"Uh-oh," I said. "Another Italian from New York in Miami. That usually means trouble." I walked to the window and looked out at the St. Johns River, the sunlight glistening on the surface. I could feel the warmth of the sun through the glass. "So, what's Canzano got to do with anything?"

"Well, he was working there when he was convicted. The article I found isn't clear. Canzano didn't get in any kind of trouble, from what I can see."

I looked outside, thinking about Brock, and if there was something more to what he wanted. There usually was.

Alex walked up behind me. "So, did he tell you what it's about?"

"He's looking for a woman, name's Jillian Rogers. But he wouldn't tell me why, or what he had to do with her. So I told him I couldn't help."

"You did?" she said. "Why?"

I turned to Alex. "Why *what*?"

"Why'd you tell him you won't help him?"

I had to think about it, and wondered if I needed to give Brock the stiff-arm the way I did. "I was probably a bit harder on Brock than I needed to be, but he likes to play games. That's how he rolls."

"*How he rolls*?" she said, with a crooked smile. "Since when did you start saying *that*?"

"I'm just saying... He's not someone I'd trust to be straight with me," I said. "I can't imagine it's worth the trouble, whatever he wants with this woman."

Alex paused, like she was thinking. "Is he still down there?"

"At Billy's?" I shook my head. "I think he left. I saw a car leave I assumed was his. But I didn't see him behind the wheel, so..."

"And you let him drive? How many drinks did he have?"

I knew I'd screwed up letting him drive, and Alex was going to make sure I knew it.

"I gave him my card, told him to call me if he decides to talk. I started up the stairs and when I looked back, he was gone. I didn't think he'd take off like he did."

Alex just shook her head, clearly disapproving.

I continued, "He seemed all right. Not many people can handle booze the way Brock can."

Alex rolled her eyes. She wasn't impressed, and I felt like a fool for even saying it, like I'd reverted back to being the same idiot I was when I considered Brock a friend.

She went back to her desk and sat in front of the laptop. "So, this woman, Jillian... What's her last name?"

"Rogers," I said.

Alex started typing.

"I don't think we should waste our time," I said. "Not unless he calls me again. He wasn't even sure she was up here."

"Then why's he here looking for her?" Alex said.

I shrugged. "I have no idea. That's why I told him I wouldn't help unless he gave me some answers."

Alex looked like she understood. "I have a hard time believing you're not the least bit curious what it's about," she said.

"He has my number," I said. "If he really wants my help, he'll call me."

Alex started typing again, then stopped, her eyes fixed on the laptop's screen. "As of this morning, there's a Jillian Rogers who lives in Miami…" She turned and looked up at me. "She's dead."

·········

Mike Stone, a detective with the Jacksonville Sheriff's Office, stood alone under the Java Jazz sign with his eyes on his phone. He had a cigarette in his mouth and looked like he tried to hide it when he saw Alex approach, holding it behind his back, then dropping it. He stomped it out.

"Didn't you say you quit," Alex said.

He shrugged. "A few times."

Alex had known Mike for a long time, and although at one point, when I first met him, I was somewhat annoyed by their relationship, I knew he was more like an uncle to her than anything else. He watched out for her. And she watched out for him.

Overall, Mike was a good guy, a somewhat grizzled, old-school detective.

He had a folder tucked under his arm and handed it to Alex. "Here's all I could get so far." He nodded toward a black steel table with an umbrella, within the roped-off sidewalk seating area outside the cafe. "Are we sitting out here?"

Alex and I both nodded, and we all stepped over the rope.

I needed a coffee, and offered to go inside to get them. Mike pulled out his wallet and tried to hand me a bill, but I shook him off.

"I got it," I said. Buying his coffee was the least I could do, considering he'd dropped whatever he was doing and made some calls, to find out what he could about the death of Jillian Rogers.

I stood in line inside, with six people already ahead of me. The woman at the front of the line was taking her time, apparently having trouble deciding what to order, as if she couldn't have figured it out before she got to the counter.

"The Girl from Ipanema" played in the background. My father always liked jazz; the older stuff, of course. And the older I got, the more respect I had for it. What's funny, was the last time I spoke with him, he'd mentioned Astrud Gilberto, the Brazilian samba and bossa nova singer behind "The Girl from Ipanema." She'd just died the day Dad and I talked, and there it was, her most famous song coming through the speakers at Java Jazz.

The woman at the front of the line finally ordered, and it felt like another ten minutes before I at last made it to the counter.

I ordered two black coffees and the mint green tea Alex wanted.

The kid behind the counter, long hair tied up in back and earrings attached to places they maybe shouldn't be, rang me up at the register. "Eighteen seventy-nine," he said.

"Eighteen seventy-nine?" I said. "Are you sure?" I looked up at the menu behind him, trying to locate some prices on the cluttered chalkboard menu. The price for anything was almost impossible to find, buried somewhere with another hundred or so items, half in a coffee-aficionado language I'd never understand.

The kid nodded, assuredly, already looking past me for the next customer in line. He had what looked like a forced smile. "It's eighteen seventy-nine, sir."

At least the kid was polite. And I knew out of that eighteen dollars he was getting a half a buck of it in wages, if he was lucky.

I pulled out a twenty and handed it to him, and he looked at the bill before he grabbed it as if he'd never seen cash before. He handed me a small card with a web address on it. "We have an app you can download for next time, so you can order and pay ahead if you'd like."

I took the card, and wondered what was wrong with my cash, the kid almost acting like it was no good.

"Keep the change," I said, wondering if he'd even know what to do with it.

I tried to carry all three tall paper cups, holding them together between my hands. Hot tea and coffee dripped onto my hand, and I did what I could to ignore it until I made it out to the table.

An older gentleman was on his way inside and held the door open for me.

"Thank you," I said, carrying our drinks to the table where Alex was seated. Mike was on the sidewalk, on the other side of the roped-off seating area, with his back to us, using his phone.

"What's going on?" I said to Alex. I placed the three cups down, rubbing the spot on my knuckle where the hot water had burned my skin. My eyes were on Mike.

"I don't know," Alex said. "He'd started to tell me what he's been able to find out about Jillian Rogers, but then he took a call. He's been on it the whole time you were inside."

"You know who it is?" I said.

Alex shook her head, then opened the folder Mike had given her and pushed it toward me. "There's no official cause of death yet," she said.

I looked inside the folder, saw the description on top of Jillian Rogers: Thirty-eight years old, five-feet-nine inches tall, no weight listed. She had blue eyes and dark brown hair. There was a black-and-white printout of her photo, Jillian Rogers smiling for the camera. She appeared to be with someone else who was cut from the photo. I flipped the sheet and saw laser-printed black-and-whites from the crime scene. She was fully clothed, dressed in shorts and what looked like a T-shirt, with bare feet, lying on a carpeted floor next to a couch. There was no blood or clear signs of trauma, from what I could see in the photo.

I glanced over at Mike and, with my voice hushed, said to Alex, "You didn't tell him anything about how I know Brock, did you?"

She shook her head.

My phone in my pocket buzzed. I looked at the screen and it was a 305 area code. Miami. I was about to answer, but tapped the ignore button instead. It could have been Brock, but I didn't want to take the call right then, in front of Mike.

Alex watched me slip the phone back into my pants pocket. "Who was it?"

I shrugged and shook my head. "I don't know."

Alex sipped her tea, looking back at me over the top like she didn't believe it.

Mike finally got off the phone and stepped over the rope without a word at first, reaching for one of the two coffees. We both drank our coffee black, and he didn't bother to ask if it mattered which cup he took.

He had a look on his face like he was thinking something through before he'd speak, placing the coffee in front of him without prying open the plastic top. He looked at Alex. "Did you look through those files?"

Alex nodded. "There's not much here."

Mike said, "Well, there've been some updates since I received these preliminary reports," he said, holding up his phone. "That was a friend of mine, down in Miami. At first it appeared Jillian Rogers death might've been some kind of freak accident. Or maybe a drug overdose. But the latest assumption is homicide."

Alex and I sat without responding.

Mike sipped his coffee, then placed the cup down, taking his time. "They're looking for a male suspect, apparently had a relationship with her."

"Does he have a name?" I said, afraid of—but knowing in my gut—what Mike's answer was going to be.

"Coincidentally, he's from up here," he said. "Ex-con, used to live up here in Jacksonville. Name sounds familiar, to be honest, but—"

"Any chance his name's Brock Mason?" I said.

Mike was in the middle of another sip of coffee but appeared to almost choke on it when I said Brock's name. He wiped his chin and looked at Alex, then at me. "Please don't tell me you two are somehow involved in any of this."

Chapter 4

I WAITED UNTIL WE were back at the house before I dialed the number from the call I'd received at Java Jazz Cafe. I wasn't sure it was the right thing to do. After telling Mike what I could about Brock, at least what I knew up to that point, I ended up practically defending him, telling Mike—with little certainty—that Brock couldn't have had anything to do with Jillian Rogers' death.

But the fact there was a space in time between when Jillian Rogers had apparently died, and when Brock had come to see me, made me think he didn't have what's considered a perfect alibi. Far from it. Take away the five-and-a-half-hour drive up to Jacksonville and the two hours he'd spent at Billy's Place, there was always a chance he'd been in Miami that morning and certainly the day before.

I tapped the recent calls I'd received and the number dialed. It rang five or six times before an automated message came on, reciting the phone number I'd called:

The person you have called...

I hung up, knowing just because it wasn't Brock's voice on the recording didn't mean he wasn't the one who had called.

I watched Alex outside on the front lawn, tossing the tennis ball for Raz. I looked at my phone, about to dial the same number again. But before I did, my phone buzzed, the call coming from the same number.

I answered right away, but didn't speak a word at first. I listened, and could hear what sounded like wind in the background.

"Hank?" the voice said.

It was him.

"Brock?" I said. "Where are you?"

"Just listen," he said. "I didn't have anything to do with Jillian's death."

"I'm supposed to believe you?"

"I was hoping you would."

I heard the front door open and walked out the back door onto the deck before Alex could see I was on the phone. I kept my voice low and said to Brock, "The cops are looking for you."

"I know."

"If you're innocent," I said, "you need to talk to them."

"I *am* innocent, Hank. I had nothing to do with it. I swear."

I could already feel it in my bones I was about to get sucked into something I'd regret. "If you didn't do it, then who did?"

He paused. "I don't know."

Alex called out to me from inside the house.

"Why did you come up here looking for her? Was she ever even here? Or was this your way of having an alibi?"

"Come on, man. I'm telling you the truth. I didn't do it."

"Then you should've come clean with me, tell me what it was about in the first place. Now, here you are. You expect me to believe you?"

"I was told she was up there."

I thought about what he'd said. "Up there? You're not in Jacksonville?"

Another pause.

"I drove here, to Miami, late last night, as soon as I heard what happened."

We were both quiet; the only thing coming through the phone was whatever sounded like wind.

"Are you in your car?" I said.

"Yeah."

"Can you close your window?"

He didn't answer, but the windlike sound had stopped.

"You need to go to the cops," I said. "It doesn't look good. And it makes it hard for me to believe you know nothing about what happened to this woman, when you're not willing to—"

"I can't. Not until I know more. I go to the cops, they're going to try to pin it on me. That's what they're looking to do, Hank."

"I don't have much information," I said. "Just what I've heard through someone I know, works up here for the sheriff's office. But there must be a reason they'd jump this fast, believing you had something to do with it."

"I guess things got a little messy between us."

"Messy?" I said. "What's that supposed to mean?"

The line went quiet.

"Brock?"

"Hank, man. You gotta help me."

"If you can't be honest with me, how do you expect me to—"

"They're going to pin this on me. You want to see your old buddy behind bars?"

"Again, you mean?" I said.

More silence.

"That was all a misunderstanding. I got involved with some people I shouldn't have, and I'm the one ends up paying the piper."

The door behind me opened and Alex stepped outside, looking me over.

I took the phone from my ear and pressed it against my chest. I said to Alex, "Can you give me a minute?"

She stood, staring at me, a suspicious look on her face. But she didn't ask who it was, instead turning and walking back into the house without a word. The door clicked as she closed it, gently, and I couldn't help but think she knew exactly who I was talking to.

I walked to the edge of the deck and leaned against the railing, overlooking the fenced-in backyard. I said to Brock, "I can't get involved. I'm at a different place now. And, whatever it is you're caught up in..."

"Hank, please."

I said, "If you'd been straight with me from the start, maybe it'd be a different story." I looked through the window at Alex pouring herself a cup of tea, Raz spread out on the floor in front of her like he was wiped out from a few rounds of fetch under the hot sun.

I was at a point in my life where things were different from what they'd ever been. I was happy, for the most part. And

I didn't want to ruin what I had. Being involved with Brock certainly meant there'd be a good chance I'd do exactly that.

"I know how this all looks," he said. "But you gotta believe me. I was looking for her because I knew she took off for a reason. At least I thought she did."

"You thought she did what?"

"Oh, yeah, uh... I mean, when she took off from Miami."

"You knew she was in trouble?" I said. "Then why didn't you go to the cops? That's the part I'm not understanding."

Brock didn't answer right away.

But then he said, "Oh no."

"Oh no what?"

"Oh shit, Hank, I—"

Hank's voice became muffled and distant, but I could hear him:

"No, please. Come on guys. You don't have to—"

Then a loud *pop*.

It was a gunshot, so loud I imagined it inches from the phone.

I listened for a moment. I could hear voices, but couldn't make out any words. I said, "Brock?" A lot of noise on the other end followed, mostly muffled, then a cracking sound.

Then silence.

I looked at my phone.

The call ended, and I dialed the number Brock had called from. But it went to the same voicemail:

The person you have reached at....

I ran into the house.

Alex was sipping from a mug, and turned to me. She frowned, one hand on her hip. "You really had to go outside to sneak your call. Was it him?"

I nodded.

"Are you okay?" she said. She could see it in my face.

"I heard a gunshot."

"A gunshot? Outside?"

"No." I held up my phone, as if she could see or hear what I already had. "Through the phone. I think someone shot him."

Alex's eyes widened. She put down her mug. "Are you sure? Do you... Where is he?"

"I don't know. In his car. Miami."

"He's not up here?" she said.

I couldn't think straight, looking at my phone, then tapping Brock's number on the screen to call him again. I put the phone on speaker and listened, but it went right to the same voicemail.

Alex put her mug down and looked around the kitchen, grabbing her phone from the counter. "Should I call Mike?"

I didn't know what to say. "I... I don't know. I don't even know where he was."

"Mike can make a call," she said.

We'd already explained to him what we knew about Brock and the deceased woman, so I had little to hide. I thought about it, and nodded. "Okay," I said. "I guess. I don't know what else to do."

I felt useless. I didn't want to help Brock at first. But this had quickly gone in a much different direction.

Alex called Mike and I walked outside onto the deck again, as if I'd find an answer out there. I felt an overwhelming sense of guilt, for turning my back on Brock.

I walked back inside and stepped over Raz, walked out of the kitchen and upstairs to our bedroom. I heard Alex on the phone, leaving a message for Mike to call her.

First thing I did was grab my duffel bag, tossing it on the bed. I started throwing clothes inside it without much thought. A few pair of boxers, some T-shirts, shorts, a tube of toothpaste and my toothbrush...

Alex stood leaning inside the doorway. "You can't go down there," she said, the phone in her hand.

I zippered the duffel bag and hung it over my shoulder without responding, trying to walk past her.

But she grabbed my arm. "Henry, slow down. Take a breath. You can't just jump in the Jeep and drive down to Miami. You have no idea what happened. You said it yourself, that you know nothing about this man."

"I know he asked for my help."

Alex held her gaze on me, then looked at her phone. "Mike's not calling back. We need to call the police. In Miami."

"And tell them what? I was on the phone with a murder suspect and heard a gunshot through the phone?"

She nodded. "Why *wouldn't* you just tell the truth?"

I pulled my arm from her and stepped outside the bedroom. I stood in the hall, my brain going a mile a minute. I hadn't thought anything through.

Alex was in the doorway, holding her phone out toward me. "We have to call the police."

I felt in my pocket for my own phone, but I wasn't even sure where I'd left it. I stepped past her and into the bedroom, walked into the bathroom, and picked it up off the counter.

I looked at myself in the mirror, the sun coming at me through the window to my left. I gazed at the phone, unsure what to do. But Alex was right. She usually was.

Chapter 5

A week had passed since I last heard from Brock. The thought had crossed my mind it could've been another one of his games, where he'd decided to use me—twice, perhaps—to set himself up with not only a potential alibi when he came up to Jacksonville to see me, but also when a shot had allegedly been fired when he'd called me.

But even for Brock Mason, it was a little much. The trouble was I hadn't stopped hearing his voice in my head, asking for my help.

With no body or evidence or a sign of some kind of foul play—his car nowhere to be found—it seemed to me his name was simply added to the long list of missing persons in the state of Florida. Twelve hundred fifty-two missing persons in the Sunshine State. At least according to statistics.

Make that twelve hundred fifty-three.

I'd been around long enough to know how these things worked. A middle-aged ex-con with a record didn't normally get the same attention a missing kid or a woman might. Ask any detective and you'll hear every case is a priority. But that's not the truth. It's just not possible. Throw in some red tape and a few dozen open cases piled on every cop's desk, and anyone can see why there are a couple hundred thousand current cold cases in the US alone.

On the other hand, all those unsolved crimes kept a guy like me in business.

Alex had gone out of town, up for a planned trip to Virginia to see her parents and spend some time with her mother. I didn't get the details of her trip, but I didn't mind having the place to myself.

I did, however, promise Alex I wouldn't take off for Miami. But I'd be lying if I said it hadn't been on my mind for the past several days.

My nights had been sleepless, to a point it even crossed my mind to go stay on my boat to see if I could get some rest. For one reason or another, lying on that crummy mattress on the boat, mildew smells and all, was like rocking a baby to sleep. At least for me it was. The water... the cabin's loud, cranky air conditioner that barely worked... I found it all quite calming.

I was at the table in the kitchen with the laptop out, having a coffee when my phone buzzed from somewhere nearby. I wasn't sure where I'd left it, and got up to look for it. I went into the other room, but the buzzing stopped.

We had a landline in the house we never used. But it was good for when I couldn't find my phone, and went over to call my cell. But before I had a chance to dial, the buzzing started again. I went back into the living room and over to the couch. The sound grew louder, and I found the phone shoved between the cushion and the arm of the couch.

I looked at the screen and saw the Miami area code, then answered, "Walsh Investigations."

"Henry?"

It was a woman's voice. It didn't take me more than a second to know who it was, although she sounded different. Older, maybe.

"Kathy?"

"It's been a long time," she said.

I couldn't remember the last time I'd heard her voice. I was close to asking Brock about her when he met me and Alex at Billy's restaurant. But I thought it was a subject best left alone.

"Yes, it has," I said. "Listen, I'm... I'm sorry I didn't call you. About Brock. I know I should have, but..."

"I understand," she said.

The line went quiet.

"No. Really. I'm sorry," I said. "I mean, to be honest, I wasn't sure if I should get involved. The cops are on top of it, right?" I felt a sense of guilt for saying something I wasn't sure I believed. I said, "When was the last time you talked to him?"

"It's been a while," she said. "Did you know he was in prison?"

"I heard."

"Well, he didn't come around much after he got out," she said. "He and my husband weren't exactly best buds."

"You're married?"

"That's how I have a husband," she said. "Five years now."

"Good guy?" I said, for no other reason than I didn't know what else to say.

She paused. "He's handsome. And he's got a lot of money. What more could I ask for?"

I had a feeling there was plenty more she could ask for. Of course, it wasn't my place to say it. "I'm glad you found someone who makes you happy."

"He reminds me a lot of you," she said.

I said, "Minus the rich and handsome part?"

She laughed, but cut it short with a sigh. "What are we supposed to do about Brock?" she said. "I can't just sit around like this."

"*We*?" I said, thinking about it for a moment, before I said something I'd regret. "What have they told you so far?"

"The cops? I'm sure you know they were looking for him already, right? Before this happened?"

"I know all about it," I said. "That's why he called me. He swore he had nothing to do with it."

"You sound like you don't believe him?"

"Brock's not the easiest guy to believe," I said.

She didn't respond.

I said, "Did you know her?"

"No, not really."

I said, "I'm sure you know how it looks, right? His girlfriend, or whatever she was, is found dead. But he's coincidentally up here to visit a friend when it allegedly happened? Something doesn't sound right."

"Brock would never kill anyone," she said.

"I didn't say he would. I'm just telling you the way they're looking at it right now. But I do know what I heard on that phone. If he is alive, I'm sure he's in some kind of trouble."

"Would you help him if he was?" she said.

"What kind of question is that?" I said, even though I didn't give her an answer. I looked out the window toward the front of the house. The sky was starting to cloud over, thunder rolling somewhere in the distance. "What do you want me to do?" I said. "I'm up here. I live in Fernandina Beach now. With my fiancée."

"Your fiancée?" she said. "You said you'd never get married again, after your wife left you. Isn't that what you told me?"

I didn't respond.

Kathy said, "What's her name?"

"Alex." I looked at my watch. I wasn't about to get into my personal life with her. I said, "Listen, I can make some calls if you'd like, see what else I can find out."

"I told Luke about you."

"Luke?" I said.

"Oh, uh... My husband."

"You told him *what* about me."

"Not about us," she said, followed by a slight laugh. "He knows you're an old friend of Brock's, and the person who called the cops about the phone call after you heard the gunshot. I told him how you were a detective, or... a private investigator."

"What did he say?"

"Other than he thinks private investigators are all hacks? Nothing."

It wasn't the first time I'd heard it. But the truth was, it couldn't have been further from the truth. A good number of PIs came from law enforcement, as I had. Most didn't take a dozen years in between to get their lives straightened out, as I did, but I'm not sure it made much of a difference.

I wasn't about to try to defend myself to Kathy, and wasn't even sure why she had to tell me what her husband said. And at that point, I'd already decided I didn't like the guy.

Kathy said, "Luke didn't think it made any sense for me to hire you."

She said it like I wouldn't have a say in the matter.

"I'm not sure I can do that," I said.

"Do what? Help? But, I can get you the money, if that's what—"

"It's not about the money," I said.

There was a long pause. "Brock... He needs your help."

What struck me as odd is the fact she seemed to've made up her mind that he was still alive. Maybe he was. But something didn't seem right, like there was something she knew but wasn't telling me.

I wouldn't say Kathy was nearly as untrustworthy as Brock. But they fell from the same tree. "How about I see what I can do from up here, make a few calls? I can get some answers."

"That's it?" she said. "You'll make a few calls? I thought Brock was your friend?"

There she was, the same Kathy trying to guilt me into something I didn't want to do. She hadn't changed.

Of course, I hadn't even thought through who I'd actually call. It wasn't like I had contacts in Miami. I mean, I knew people. Or, I should say, I knew people who knew people.

"How much do you need?" she said.

"I already told you, this isn't about the money."

Of course, whether she'd pay me or not wasn't going to help me decide one way or the other to go all the way down to Miami and get involved in something my gut told me I shouldn't.

However, I of course had to consider the fact that business had slowed quite a bit over the past few months, to a point where work was almost nonexistent. Alex and I were doing some things to get Walsh Investigations back on track.

I thought, for a moment, I could try to convince myself—and Alex—I'd do it for the money. Make it all about business.

I said, "Let me call you later. Tonight, probably. I'd need to consult with my partner."

"Your partner? I didn't know you—."

"Alex, my fiancée. She's also my business partner."

There was another few seconds of silence on the phone.

"Okay," Kathy said. "Do what you have to do. But don't blow me off."

"I won't." I said, and glanced at the number on my phone. "Is this the best number to reach you? The one you called from?"

"Yes. But if I don't answer, don't leave a message. I'll call you back."

"Don't leave a message?" I said, making sure I heard what she said. I wasn't sure why.

"I'll see your number," she said. "I'll call you back. Bye for now, Henry." She hung up without another word.

Chapter 6

THE HANDFUL OF PEOPLE at the bar turned to watch me walk into Billy's Place. I didn't recognize anyone, a different crowd than it was during my drinking days.

Billy was behind the bar, toward the back of it, facing the other direction when I sat down. He glanced at me over his shoulder. "Lonely?" He smiled, went back to whatever he was doing.

He had a pen in his hand, standing by the register with the drawer open, making notes on a pad. He closed the drawer and walked over to me.

"Did you talk to her?" he said.

"Who, Alex?"

Billy cracked a smile, nodding. "Yeah, of course." He turned and glanced up at the clock. "I don't remember the last time you've been in here this late."

I looked toward the far end of the bar where an older couple acted like teenagers, snugged up against each other.

Billy rolled his eyes. "I wish they'd stop that."

I smiled. "You got any coffee made?"

"I'll make you some," he said, turning for the door to the kitchen.

"No, that's all right," I said, my eyes on the bottles on the back wall behind him. I couldn't remember the last drink I had. But I wasn't one for counting the days, or making that last drink some kind of special date I had to remember. "I'll have a ginger ale."

He stepped back toward me, hands resting on the bar. He leaned in, getting a good look at me. "You all right?"

I wasn't sure, and didn't answer. "I just got a call from Kathy Mason. Brock's sister. You remember her?"

"Kathy?" he said, eyebrows raised, nodding. "You haven't talked to her since—"

"I never called her. I don't know why... I wish I had. I guess it's just... It's been a long time."

Billy nodded, like he wasn't sure what to say, then reached for a glass from the brass rack over his head. He poured me a soda and tossed a coaster in front of me, placing the glass on top of it. "Does Alex know about Kathy?"

I said, "I didn't mention anything to her. It's not a big deal."

Billy had a look on his face like he wanted to smile. "You sure?"

"Sure what?"

"It's not a big deal?"

I held on to the glass, about to take a drink, but kept it there, thinking.

"Let me make you some coffee," Billy said. He walked through the swinging door to the kitchen.

I pulled out my phone and looked at the screen to see if Alex had called. Turns out she'd sent a text an hour earlier, but I'd missed it.

She wrote,

Good night. I'm going to bed.

I tapped a reply:

Sorry, just saw this now. Talk to you in the morning?

She didn't respond.

The door from the kitchen swung open and Billy walked through carrying a cup of coffee on a saucer. "Chloe had already made a fresh pot," he said, placing the cup in front of me. He took the glass of soda from the bar and dumped it in the sink.

"Thanks," I said.

Billy said, "I assume she called about Brock?"

"Kathy?" I said, taking a sip of the hot coffee, looking at him over the rim. I nodded. "She wants my help. But I told her I'd see what I can find out. I'm not going to Miami. Not right now."

Billy had a look on his face, like he knew there was something I wasn't telling him.

"But you're thinking about it?" he said. "I mean, he's an old friend. And, now your ex-girlfriend is calling you?"

"Alex would never go for it," I said.

"Because you'd have to go to Miami? Or because it's your ex-girlfriend who wants you down there."

"You know Alex wouldn't care about some woman from my past."

"But you didn't say anything to her? That you were involved with Brock's sister?"

I shook my head and shrugged. "What's there to say?"

Billy rolled his eyes. "Are you kidding? You know why. She'll think you've got something to hide," he said. "That's the part she won't like."

"Yeah, of course. I know."

Billy said, "Then why wouldn't you just tell her?"

I didn't have a good answer, and didn't respond. I took a sip of coffee. "She wants to hire me."

Billy paused. "Then why not take it, treat it like a job?"

"I guess it depends on how you look at it," I said. "If he's alive, then he's hiding and doesn't want to be found. Nobody even knows if he's in Miami."

"Then you make some money trying to find him," Billy said. "Treat her like a client. But I know how you are. You come up empty-handed, you won't take the money."

"I'm not sure that's true," I said, although it probably was.

Billy said, "You can't survive as a businessman because you feel funny charging friends. Besides, hasn't it been long enough between you two?"

I looked at my phone to see if Alex had responded to my last text. She hadn't. "I guess I'll talk to Alex about it, see what she thinks." I got up from the stool and tossed a couple bills on the bar.

Billy picked up the money and handed it back to me. "Where're you going?"

I grabbed the coffee. "Mind if I bring this with me up to the office?"

· · · • · • • • · ·

I sipped my cold coffee, seated at my desk with the laptop open in front of me. With the overhead lights off, the only light came from the laptop's screen.

There was little information online about Brock Mason online. Trackers, the service we used to track someone down, with 120 billion records, came up dry, other than a couple of small loan defaults Brock had tied to his name.

The most recent piece of news included my name along with Brock's, assuming I was the "friend from Jacksonville" who reported him missing and possibly a victim of an alleged shooting. There was little detail, and it appeared the local media in Miami took it about as seriously as the cops had.

Brock had no presence on social media. I couldn't really fault him for that, however. I didn't either.

Alex, though, had tried to persuade me to "put myself out there" and promote the business. Like I told her, I'm a private investigator. Nobody was interested in hearing what I had to say, and I wasn't about to put my ugly mug in front of a few million strangers, like I was some kind of celebrity. That stuff was for kids, the way I saw it.

The one thing I had in common with any of these social media weirdos—influencers, I guess they were called—was that I still lived in my parents' house.

I pulled up the *Miami Post*'s article Alex had found the night Brock showed up looking for me. It was a pretty in-depth article about what appeared to be some kind of charity fraud scheme. Brock was barely mentioned.

My phone buzzed on my desk. It was a text from Alex:

Are you awake?

I tapped her number and called her.

"Hey," she said when she answered, almost in a whisper, as if she'd been asleep. "Were you sleeping?"

"Not at all," I said.

There was a pause.

"Are you home?" she said, as if she already knew I wasn't.

I hesitated at first. But lying would've made no sense. "I'm at the office."

"The office? Are you... It's after midnight. Why? What are you doing?"

I figured I'd deflect her question. "Are you okay?" I said.

"I'm good. Yes. I just can't sleep."

"Me neither," I said. "I don't think I've slept since you left."

"Because you miss me?" she said. I could hear her smile.

"Well, of course. But..."

"Because of Brock?" she said.

I wasn't sure if I needed to tell her about Kathy's call. Or, more specifically, about who Kathy was. But not telling her would be a mistake, as Billy pointed out. As I'd often learned the hard way, Alex is much smarter than me. There's very little I could hide from her.

And I knew I had no reason good enough to keep anything from her.

"I got a call from Brock's sister," I said.

"His sister? I didn't see anything about a sister," she said. "Do you know her?"

"You could say that."

Alex paused on the other end, then said, "What's *that* supposed to mean, 'you could say that?'"

I cleared my throat and stood up from the desk, walking across the darkness in our office toward the window. I looked out at the moon's glow on the St. Johns. "She wants to hire me—us—to find Brock. Or, find out what happened to him."

The line went quiet again.

"Do you trust her?" Alex said.

"Well, that's another question," I said.

"Would she be a real client? Or is she hoping just because you're an old friend of her brother's, you'll work for free?"

I sat on the couch in front of the window and lay down. Talking to Alex helped me relax. Maybe she was right. Maybe my lack of sleep was because I missed her.

I said, "She made it sound like her husband and Brock didn't get along."

"Oh, so she's married," she said. "I guess that's good, right?"

"I don't know. Sure. He's got money. And he's handsome."

"Is that what she told you?"

"In those exact words," I said.

There was another moment of silence on the phone.

Alex said, "So how'd you leave it with her?"

"I told her I had to talk to you."

"I assume this means you'd be going to Miami?"

I said, "You mean *we'd* be going to Miami."

Alex paused. "I can't. I'm here to visit my parents. They need my help with some things."

"Oh, okay," I said.

"I can do what I can to help from here," she said. "Just promise me you'll stay out of trouble."

Chapter 7

I turned left off Northwest Seventy-First onto Biscayne Boulevard, and turned right into Johnny's Eastside Diner. After I'd told Billy I had agreed I should take the so-called job, he didn't like the idea of me driving my old Jeep down to Miami. It ran fine, but wasn't exactly made for long trips. So he'd offered me one of his cars, and I ended up driving down in an older BMW Billy had recently picked up at the auction.

He had a thing for buying nice cars on the cheap, especially older luxury models like BMWs and Mercedes. He'd either keep them as part of his collection—he had about fifteen cars in a garage he built to store them—or he'd have them refurbished so he could sell them for more than what he paid. Buying cars was somewhat of a hobby of his, but he also seemed to have multiple streams of income on top of owning his restaurant. He certainly knew how to make money, something I wouldn't say was exactly in my wheelhouse.

I stepped out and looked around the mostly empty parking lot, save for six or seven cars parked toward the back. They were under shade from two small, live oaks somehow growing out of a narrow strip of vegetation surrounded by hot asphalt that had lifted from the trees' roots. It was past lunchtime, and I guessed the cars belonged to the employees. But there was a white Mercedes that stood out, only the front end of it getting any shade.

Inside the diner was as empty as the parking lot. I turned to my left, looking all the way toward the last booth. Kathy sat, watching me, until a smile took over her face as she stood and started toward me.

It had been a long time, but Kathy didn't look much different from the last time I saw her. She was tan, hair darker than I remembered. I was used to Alex and her nearly six-foot frame, so when Kathy was finally right in front of me, her arms outstretched, I was surprised—I guess I'd forgotten—she was quite a bit shorter than me.

"Look at you," she said, staring up at me like an old aunt you hadn't seen in a long time, telling you how much you've grown.

We hugged, but I made it quick and backed away when it felt like she was about to try to plant a kiss on my cheek.

The smile was plastered on her face, and she gazed back at me without saying a word. "I'm so happy to see you," she said.

I grinned.

Her big smile made me feel somewhat uncomfortable, considering the situation.

"Are you hungry?" she said, turning toward the table. "I know how much you like diners, figured you'd like it here. We have the whole place to ourselves."

I wasn't sure where she got the idea I was someone who had some kind of deep passion about eating in diners, but I didn't try to correct her. Maybe she mixed me up with someone else, although I guess she wasn't that far off. I certainly preferred a simple place to eat over some fancy, upscale joint.

I followed her back to the booth where we both slid in, on opposite sides, neither saying a word for a couple of moments like we didn't know who should say what first.

"Why didn't your partner come?" she said, picking up a tall clear glass with a lime inside. She took a sip, watching me.

I told her how Alex was at her parents' house up in Virginia, and that she'd already planned to spend time with them for a couple of weeks.

The waitress came over and asked me if I wanted a drink.

"Coffee, please," I said.

The waitress pointed with her pen at the menus stacked in the rack with the silver napkin holder. "Today's specials are inside the menu."

Kathy leaned back, arms straight out, her drink between both hands. She didn't say much at first, staring at me in a way that made me uneasy.

Kathy was different from her brother. But they were also similar, and not in a good way.

"So, what have you heard?" I said. "From the police, or..."

"I haven't heard a thing," she said. She lowered her voice and leaned forward. "I don't think this is the right place for us to talk."

I looked around the empty diner, noticing only one waitress doing much of anything; the other two I could see eating together at one of the tables at the far end from where we sat, on the other side of the diner. "Then why'd you want me to meet you here?"

"Well, we're going to go for a ride, after you put some food in your belly. I know how you get when you don't eat."

For some reason, it seemed now as if she wouldn't look me in the eye.

"What's going on?" I said, my suspicions starting to grow.

She looked up at me and grinned, but I could see the seriousness behind her fraudulent smile. "Nothing. Just... just be patient. I promise, I'll tell you what I can."

The waitress brought over my coffee and placed it in front of me, along with a small, silver creamer I didn't need. "Would you like to order something to eat?"

I got the feeling the young woman either needed to sell us some food, or was in a hurry to get out of there. Maybe her shift was about to end.

"Just bring me the check," I said.

"Oh, uh, okay." She pulled a pad from her smock, tore off the sheet on top, and placed it on the table. "Whenever you're ready."

I pulled my wallet out of my back pocket and looked at the bill:

"Twenty-three dollars?" I said. I looked at Kathy's drink and said to her, "What are you drinking?"

"Vodka tonics," she said, smiling.

"I've never been to a diner that serves booze," I said.

She shrugged. "One of the few that do." She drank whatever was left in the glass, then pushed it forward. "I got here early."

I left cash on the table and got up without finishing my coffee, waiting for Kathy to go ahead of me. "I drove too far to play games, Kathy, so whatever you're up to..."

She stepped from the table and gave me a quick look on her way by, that sly smile of hers, and continued to the exit.

I slipped my sunglasses over my eyes as soon as we stepped outside, reaching for Kathy's arm. "Wait," I said. "Listen, I'm not going anywhere with you until you tell me what this is all about."

She had sunglasses on now herself, and pulled them down to look at me over the top. "Can't you just trust me?" she said, looking around the lot. "Can you drive?" she said. "I might've had too much to drink."

I didn't like how she continued to ignore me. "I'm not going anywhere until you tell me where we're going?"

She was still for a moment, then let out a sigh, looking around once again before she finally nodded. "It's Brock. He needs to talk to you."

I lowered my head and closed my eyes behind my sunglasses, taking a deep breath to stop myself from losing it. I started to walk away, heading toward my car, then stopped. I tried to contain my frustration. "I knew it," I said, throwing up my arms. I walked toward the BMW, keys in my hand. "I'm such an idiot. I should've never—"

I was about to slide the key into the door when Kathy came up behind me, one hand around my waist, the other on my hand with the key in the door. "I'm sorry," she said. "I couldn't tell you anything over the phone. Brock made me promise. And I couldn't let Luke hear anything. He has no idea."

"Your husband?" I said. "I guess you haven't changed much, huh? Lying to anyone dumb enough to listen?"

"Brock was afraid you wouldn't come down if I told you the truth."

"You got that right," I said.

She slipped in front of me and stood between me and the driver-side door. "Henry, please. Brock's in real trouble."

"Did he kill Jillian Rogers?"

Kathy shook her head. "No. That's why he needs your help."

"Why the hell can't he just go to the cops?" I said, trying to keep my cool.

She gave me a look, like I'd asked a stupid question. "They think he killed her. And whoever did it, made sure that's how it would look." She paused. "They say they saw him leaving her apartment."

I said, "Well, that tells you something, doesn't it?"

She looked as if she couldn't give me a straight answer. "Please," she said, her hand on my arm. "He'll explain everything."

Chapter 8

THE FIFTEEN-MINUTE DRIVE TOOK us to a sleazy-looking motel in Miami Gardens, my eyes on the lookout for the black Dodge Charger I thought Brock had been driving. But I guessed even Brock wasn't dumb enough to park it out in the open where someone could see it.

I was still steaming from being deceived by him and his sister, but more anxious than anything to understand exactly what it was Brock had been up to, from the moment he showed up at Billy's Place looking for me.

Kathy stepped out of the car without a word, walking at a good pace ahead of me, then stopping as if waiting for me. She looked around, left and right, and continued toward the building.

The motel had two floors. A worn, rusty metal railing ran across the top level, with dirty, plastic white chairs to the side of each room's door. Some rooms had mismatched green plastic tables with the chairs.

I locked the car door and hurried to catch up with Kathy walking around the corner of the motel. She'd started up the stairs, and I ran my eyes along the doors up top, each with a single square window. The blinds moved behind one of them, and I could only assume it was Brock, watching us.

I still hadn't decided how I was going to react when I saw him. To say I was pissed off would be an understatement, but I was trying to convince myself to listen first before reacting. But I wasn't sure that was going to happen.

Kathy continued up the stairs ahead of me, got to the top exterior walkway, and stopped ahead at the door to the room where I saw the curtains move. She waited until I was closer, then knocked twice on the door. She turned before it opened, looking toward the parking lot below.

Cars drove on the street going both ways past the motel. There were a few other cars in the parking lot, maybe four or five.

The door opened, chain still across the top, Brock's face showing up from within the shadows.

He slid the chain off and Kathy walked inside, glancing back at me as she stepped across the threshold.

I walked in behind her into the dim room, lit by a small lamp with a yellow glow on the table next to the bed. The curtains were closed on the window, and it stunk like mildew and cigarettes and maybe body odor.

As far as I knew, Brock didn't smoke.

He stood in a flowered bathing suit and a plain, white T-shirt, wrinkled like he'd just taken it out of the package, and flip-flops on his feet. "Listen, Henry, I'm sorry I—"

I stepped into him and clocked him with a left, catching him in the jaw with a punch I wasn't able to hold back, no matter how much I'd tried to talk myself out of hitting him.

Kathy screamed, "Henry! No!"

Brock tried to throw a punch back at me, but I hit him again and he stumbled, falling onto the unmade bed, then onto the stained, green carpet on the floor.

"You're a goddamn liar," I said, my outstretched finger pointed toward his face. "You always were, and always will be."

I grabbed him by the arm and lifted him to his feet, throwing him onto the bed again where he sat up holding his jaw, shifting it like I'd knocked it out of place.

He wiped a spot of blood from his lip. "I did what I had to do," he said. "I'm sorry I put you in a spot, but..."

"You staged the whole thing? Just so I'd call the cops, tell them you were shot? And missing?"

"I'm sorry," he said, as if an apology would make a difference.

I yelled, "That's the best plan you could come up with? You ever think, I don't know... about just disappearing? Get out of Miami, like a normal person would do?"

Brock sat on the edge of the bed, not saying a word. He touched his lip, which had swelled up a bit after I'd whacked him.

"What about coming up to Jax?" I said. "Was that all part of your plan?"

Brock shook his head emphatically. "No! I swear, Hank. I thought... I really thought Jillian was—"

"Can you stop calling me Hank?" I said. "Nobody calls me that, like some old man working the gas pumps. I've been telling you that for I don't know how many years."

Brock swallowed hard, head tilted like a little kid who'd been scolded for saying a bad word, raising his gaze to mine as he nodded. He cracked a grin. "I always kind of like calling you that."

"Which one of you are gonna tell me what the hell's going on?" I glared at Kathy, then Brock. "Am I really supposed to believe you don't know who's after you?"

He nodded. "Why wouldn't I tell you, if I knew? I mean, I have an idea but..."

"You have a long list of people who want to harm you? Is that the problem? Bunch of 'em in line, looking to wring your neck?"

Brock didn't respond.

I said, "Come on, Brock. You're not fooling me. You must have some kind of idea what this is all about." I was starting to calm down a bit. "Does this have anything to do with that scheme you were busted for?"

He appeared as if he had to think through how to answer. "I was innocent."

"That's not my question," I said, turning to Kathy.

She just shrugged.

I said to her, "Were you involved in it too?"

"No," is all she said.

I said to Brock, "What about this guy, Giotti? You did time together?"

Brock shook his head. "I never even met him," he said. "My name was just on the paperwork, hiring some part-time help. I wasn't paying attention, you know?"

"If that was your argument in court, I could see how you did time," I said.

Kathy said, "His lawyer wasn't very good."

I looked from Kathy to Brock, not sure if either one was telling me the truth.

"What about this guy, Canzano, you were working for? How come he didn't do time?"

Brock said, "This has nothing to do with any of what happened back then." He turned from me, like he couldn't look me in the eye. "I'm sorry we lied. But we really need—"

"Can you help him?" Kathy said. "We can pay you. Nobody's looking for charity."

I didn't answer, my eyes on Brock. "So, you went through all this BS to get me down here? You couldn't just tell me the truth?"

"I wasn't thinking," Brock said. "How many times you want me to say I'm sorry?"

I took a deep breath, thinking it all through. There was a lot to swallow. "Listen," I said. "I just don't think I want to be a part of this." I looked at the wallpaper behind the bed, stained and dirty like it hadn't been wiped down in years. "I don't like any of this. Hiding in motels. Lying to so-called friends. It just doesn't sit well with me."

Kathy said. "Name your price."

I said, "You don't know me very well. It's never about the money with me."

"Everyone's gotta eat," Brock said, as if whatever vomit came out of his mouth would make a difference.

I couldn't shake the fact I knew there was something they weren't telling me. I said to Kathy, "I understand you want to help your brother. But what's in it for you?" I said to Brock, "You ever think about maybe telling the truth? Cops tend to appreciate people who shoot straight."

He paused, glanced toward the floor, then raised his gaze. "There's a reason they think I did it."

"Kathy told me," I said. "Somebody saw you at her apartment."

Brock took his time, his eyes toward the floor again, like he was thinking it all through before he said the wrong thing. "I got a call that morning, before I drove up to Jax. Someone called my cell—a private number—and told me to meet at her building."

"So you were there?" I said.

He nodded.

"Who called?" I said. "You didn't go to see Jillian?"

He shook his head. "No. I don't know who it was. I was supposed to meet them inside the garage, but there was nobody there. I walked around for a bit. Nothing. There are cameras all over the place. In the garage... outside over the parking lot, where I parked."

"So, what you're saying is they have you on camera in the building where your girlfriend was murdered?"

Brock nodded. "Somebody set me up."

I looked toward the door and ran my hand through my hair. I thought, right then, the best thing I could do was walk out and never look back. But I couldn't help myself. "So, what, you drove up to Jax, right from there?"

Brock said, "I got a call, a woman said she was a friend of Jillian's up there, asked if I knew where she was. She said she was supposed to meet her in Jax later in the afternoon."

"You know this woman's name?"

He shook his head. "No."

I said, "So, how'd she get your number?"

Brock shrugged.

"And you didn't talk to Jillian at any point that morning? Or the night before?"

He said, "I called her half a dozen times, sent her texts. She never answered."

"Because she was dead," Kathy said.

I ran my hands over my face, as if trying to clear a web I'd walked through.

This one was getting sticky.

"So, you get this call to go to the building, then another that she's up in Jacksonville? I guess what I'm not understanding is, what made you start looking for her? Was she already missing?"

Brock took a moment before he answered. "We got into an argument the day before about some things. She wasn't at her apartment that night when I went over. Like I said, she didn't answer my calls or texts."

"You didn't show your texts to the cops?"

"I deleted them," he said.

"Are you serious?" I waited, a look on his face like he had more to say, but held back. I said, "I can't do anything if you're going to leave me in the dark here."

Brock looked toward the open door to the bathroom at the back of the room. He said, "She was doing some work for Canzano."

"I thought you said it had nothing to do with what happened back then?" I said.

"It didn't. I mean, not exactly. But..." He cleared his throat, again looking toward the open bathroom door.

Kathy pulled a wooden chair from under the small desk by the door and sat down.

I said, "Is that how you met her? You both worked for Canzano?"

Brock nodded.

"But you're telling me he has nothing to do with any of this?" I said.

Brock said nothing.

I stepped over to the window, pulled the curtain aside and peeked out over the railing and into the parking lot. There was a black car parked near mine, but I couldn't see if anyone was inside it. There were plenty of spaces. And I knew the car wasn't there when we first pulled in.

I turned back to Brock and Kathy. "One of you want to look outside, see if you recognize that black sedan parked near the BMW I'm driving?"

Brock's eyes opened wide. He looked scared, walking to the window. He stopped in front of Kathy, still seated in the chair.

She stood and got to the curtain first, pulled it aside only slightly—enough to get an eye on whoever it was—then pulled it closed. "The black car?" She shook her head. "I have no idea." She seemed somewhat nonchalant about it, stepping out of the way so Brock could take a look.

He took his time, looking, but then backed away. "I don't see anything," he said.

I walked to the window and looked out there again, but the car was gone.

Kathy didn't appear too concerned. She said, "Brock, tell him about the gig."

"The gig?" I said, grinding my teeth.

Brock looked at his sister, and seemed to hesitate. "Jillian, she, uh..." He stopped, whatever it was he was about to say.

"Jillian *what*?" I said, trying to stay calm.

Brock said, "I can't go into the details just yet, but..."

I yelled, "What do you mean you can't go into the details?" I took a step toward him, ready to grab him by the neck. "What was she doing? Was she a hooker? Or..." I turned and opened the door. "I'm out of here," I said. "Good luck, buddy." I walked outside and slammed the hotel room door closed behind me.

Kathy came out after me. "Henry! Wait!"

I opened the driver-side door and Kathy went around to the passenger side. "What are you doing?" I said.

"Just open the door," she said.

Chapter 9

KATHY WAS IN THE passenger seat, neither of us saying much of anything for the first few miles after we left Brock at the motel. It was when we got to the on-ramp for 95 and saw that traffic backed up for as far as we could see it, Kathy pointed straight ahead.

"Keep going," she said. "Take Seventy-First."

I cut back into the left lane and continued past the ramp for the highway, turning instead a half mile ahead.

"Then look for Seventy-Fourth," she said. "It'll be on your left. A mile down, take Northwest Seventh." She turned from me and looked out the passenger window.

I watched her, waiting. "Can you just tell me the truth?"

It took a moment for her to turn from the window. "What makes you think I'm not being truthful?"

I laughed. "Are you serious? I'm not sure anything you've told me has an ounce of truth to it. You've lied to me since the moment I picked up the phone and you were on the other end."

She said, "Brock's trying to protect us."

I laughed again, not that any of it was funny. "Is that what he told you?"

Kathy looked ahead and yelled, "Turn here!" like she'd forgotten she was my copilot in a city I didn't know very well.

I'd pretty much forgotten whatever time I'd spent in Miami, considering it'd been so long. Getting around had always been somewhat confusing and congested for me, with far too many cars, not to mention all the people looking for the so-called Magic in Miami.

Kathy shifted in her seat, one leg tucked under the other. "So, what are your plans tonight?"

"My plans?" I shrugged. "I haven't even checked into my hotel."

I looked straight ahead, but knew she was watching me.

She said, "You're not even going to think about it?"

"Think about *what*?"

"Helping Brock?"

I gave her a quick look without answering, then shifted my eyes to the rearview mirror.

A dark sedan passed a few cars, then slid in so there was only one car between us.

My first thought was it looked like the same car I saw outside Brock's motel. I wasn't sure, however. There was no need to be paranoid, I thought. I hadn't slept well the night before. And I was hungry. Not a good combination for the brain.

But something didn't feel right. I tried to get a better look in the mirror without driving off the road or smashing into the back of the pickup truck in front of us.

I was pretty sure the car outside the motel was a Lincoln Town Car, from what I could see. I wished I'd paid better attention when I saw it at the motel.

My phone vibrated on the middle seat between me and Kathy. I picked it up and glanced at the screen. It was Alex. I don't know why, but it made me nervous with Kathy in the seat next to me, as if I was doing something wrong.

I tried to sound upbeat when I answered. "Hey! I was going to call you. How's it going?"

"I was going to ask you the same thing," she said. "I thought you said you were going to call me when you checked into the hotel?"

"I was. But I haven't checked in yet."

I looked at the clock. It was a little after four.

"You haven't checked in?"Alex said.

I looked in the rearview again.

Kathy was looking at me, and she said, "What's the matter?" She turned to look toward the rear window. "Is someone back there?"

Alex said, "Who's that?"

I didn't feel like getting into it right then. I couldn't.

"It's, uh, it's Brock's sister," I said. "Kathy."

"Oh," is all Alex said.

I waited, expecting more. But there was silence on the other end of the line.

Looking in the rearview once again, the black sedan had passed the car ahead of it and was now behind us. But the driver didn't get too close. At that point, I had little doubt it was the same vehicle from the motel.

I said to Alex, "Can I call you back? I've got something I need to deal with." I hoped the car behind us would get closer so I could at least get a look at whoever was behind the wheel.

But it appeared as if the driver was purposely hanging back to avoid my already growing suspicions.

"Can you at least tell me what you're doing?" Alex said. I could hear it in her voice she sounded somewhat displeased and maybe concerned.

"Brock is alive," I said. "But it's a long story. And right now I've got someone on my tail. I need to find out who it is."

"Someone's following you?" Alex said.

"Let me call you back. I shouldn't be driving with the phone anyway." Normally, I'd put it on speaker. It's not like on occasion I didn't act like every other idiot out there, talking on a phone while trying to drive. I knew better. But I didn't want to put Alex on speaker as I normally would. Not with Kathy next to me.

"Of course," Alex said. "Please, call me back."

I was about to hang up, but stopped when Alex said my name. I put the phone back to my ear. She said, "Promise me you'll be careful."

"Always," I said, and hung up the phone.

I placed the phone on the seat between me and Kathy and looked back through the mirror.

I said to Kathy, "Call your brother."

"Brock?"

"Do you have another one?"

She huffed. "Do you have to act like that?" She turned in her seat and looked toward the rear window again, then glanced my way. "Is that the car from the motel?"

I kept my eyes on the mirror and didn't answer, then looked ahead at the yellow traffic light about to turn red. "Hang on," I said, slamming my foot down on the gas pedal. I yanked the wheel, landing in the left oncoming lane, opposing traffic coming toward us, then jerked it back to the right. Cutting in front of the pickup truck ahead of us, the driver laid on the horn, making some gestures with his hands.

We passed the Wells Fargo on the left, where a police car was parked out front, but with no cop inside of it. "Hold tight," I said, and took a hard, sharp turn after the bank onto Seventy-Ninth.

The old Beemer didn't sound like it was up for any kind of hard driving. Billy had assured me he'd had it tuned up, as he did with all the cars he bought at the auction.

But when I came off the turn onto Seventy-Ninth and hit the gas, the engine sputtered, and didn't seem to want to go.

The black Town Car took the corner almost on two wheels and was moving at a good speed after us.

Kathy watched me, her eyes wide open, gripping the dashboard and the handle over the passenger window.

The Beemer slowed, almost to a stop, like it was going to conk out. But just as the Town Car got closer, I pumped the gas pedal and slammed my foot down. We took off so fast, the backs of both of our heads slammed against the headrest.

Black smoke came out from the tailpipe and filled the air behind us. It was as if something had nested in the muffler and needed to be coughed out.

But the Town Car was closer now, a few feet behind us. With the dark, tinted-glass windshield, I still couldn't get a good look at the driver.

The turn for Biscayne was up ahead, the Town Car right up my rear.

I knew slamming on the brakes wasn't the best option. But there was traffic stopped ahead, before turning onto Biscayne. My only option was to stay on Seventy-Ninth then onto the causeway, heading toward Miami Beach.

Kathy made a sound like she was trying to take a deep breath, but couldn't.

"Stay calm," I said.

She had her eyes fixed on the road. "What are you doing?"

"What does it look like I'm doing?" I said, without giving her much more of an answer.

Mainly, because I didn't have one.

Traffic lights were flashing ahead. "Oh no," I said.

A signal and a sign indicated the drawbridge was about to be raised. Up ahead I could see the long, gated arm with red flashing lights on it starting to come down across the road.

I repeated what I'd already said to Kathy at least a couple of times before. "Hold on!" I slammed my foot down on the gas, my eyes on the building where the drawbridge operator sat to work the drawbridge. I hoped he saw me coming and might hold off lifting the bridge. But there was also a chance he didn't see me. It wouldn't be the first time a drawbridge operator wasn't paying attention.

By then, it was too late for me to stop, going a good eighty-something miles an hour. The Town Car was still behind me, but had dropped back somewhat.

The barrier arm gate was almost all the way down, and the drawbridge had started to lift. There was no chance I'd try to pull off some Hollywood stuntman move and jump the bridge to get to the other side. Maybe if I'd been a few years younger, and more foolish than I already was…

"Please don't," Kathy said, her voice shaky. She braced herself as if I was going to do it, legs straight out with her feet placed firmly on the floor, her body pressed hard against the passenger seat's backrest. Her arms were straight out in front of her, pressing against the BMW's wood-grained dashboard.

It was too late for me to slow down. I slammed on the brakes but hit the gate, pieces of it flying everywhere as I smashed through it. I cut the wheel, tires squealing, smoke coming out from underneath. I turned so hard, two wheels came off the ground.

I hit the concrete median dividing the causeway so hard with a loud bang, it felt like the car's body had cracked. I knew right away I'd blown out the tires.

Kathy screamed as loud as I'd ever heard anyone.

We crashed down off the median and slid across three empty lanes. My eyes were on Biscayne Bay, over the railing. I cut the wheel, slid sideways, and slammed on the brakes. But I hadn't been able to slow us down enough, and we smashed into the barrier railing, the worst of it on Kathy's side. The passenger window's glass shattered, thousands of tiny bits of glass flying past Kathy as if in slow motion. The airbags exploded into our faces, slamming our heads back with such force it felt like I'd been hit by Mike Tyson, landing the final knockout blow.

We had come to a full stop, the car on the wrong side of the causeway, facing the wrong direction.

A loud hissing noise coming from the engine. I cleared the now deflated airbag out of my way. "Kathy?"

She didn't answer.

"Kathy?" I reached for her. "Are you okay?"

She was bloodied, and started to whimper. Then she cried, but not hysterically, nodding, her face a ghostlike white. Blood dripped from her mouth.

I reached out for her, ignoring my own pain and the warmth of my own blood coming down my face. I picked the glass from her hair and shoulders.

Sirens screamed in the distance, and when I looked around for the Town Car, all I saw were people on the other side of the road, most out of their cars now, some watching, some rushing toward us.

The Town Car, however, was gone.

Chapter 10

IT SEEMED THE OFFICERS from the Miami-Dade Police Department weren't convinced I was telling the truth about what had happened on the causeway. A couple of officers appeared at odds about whether or not they had reason to arrest me.

In the end, that's exactly what they did.

Kathy was taken to the hospital, although luckily appeared to have minor injuries. It didn't mean I wasn't worried about her.

With two blown tires and busted rims, on top of what looked like considerable damage to the front and side of Billy's BMW, I had little choice but to get into the back of the Miami-Dade cruiser anyway. It's just that my preference would've been to do so by my own choosing, without the handcuffs on my wrists.

By the time we made it to the station, I'd decided it wasn't worth me getting thrown behind bars to protect Brock. Besides, I knew the best thing for him, even if he didn't believe it himself, might be to have the cops on his side.

I had a white Styrofoam cup of coffee in front of me, seated at a square metal table bolted to the floor in the middle of the small windowless room. There was a video camera with a blinking red light on it, attached to the ceiling in the corner. There were no two-way mirrors, but I knew I was being watched. A round clock was the only other thing on the bare gray walls.

The excessive brightness in the room came from what I guessed were canned LED bulbs shining down from the ceiling. They were almost painful on my tired eyes. I wasn't against being eco-friendly, but I missed incandescent bulbs. To me, a burning wire inside a glass bulb was more natural.

But what did I know?

I felt a chill, with the air conditioning blowing steady from the vents on the ceiling. Even the hard metal chair I sat on was cold to the touch, so pretty uncomfortable.

I glanced at the manilla folder on the table, placed in front of the phone by the officer who led me into the room.

The door opened and a young woman I would've guessed was a college-aged kid stepped inside the room. She was tall and thin, dressed in a suit with a gold cross on a necklace around her neck, her buttoned shirt opened at the top.

"I'm Detective Collins," she said, picking up the folder and looking at whatever was inside. She kept her eyes down, flipped through the papers, then raised her gaze. "We sent a couple of officers up to the hotel. But your friend isn't there. The room was empty."

"Yeah, because whoever followed me onto the causeway knew where he was. They probably already went back and grabbed him."

She looked down at the folder again, flipped through a couple of sheets of paper, then placed the folder on the table. She pulled the chair back and sat, staying quiet for a moment or two, hands steepled in front of her. "So you're the one who reported he'd been shot, and had since been missing?"

I nodded. "I'm not the one who lied. He set it all up, so I'd come down here. He lied to me."

I didn't love the idea of telling the truth about Brock Mason. But our relationship wasn't one, any longer, where it was worth me putting my own neck on the line just to protect him. And, if he was telling the truth—that he had nothing to do with Jillian Rogers' death—then I'd do all I could to help clear his name. But, until then, I felt it was up to me to tell the truth.

Detective Collins said, "I assume you're well aware he's a suspect in a murder?"

"Of course," I said.

She leaned back in the chair, staring at me. "There's footage of him at the murder scene," she said.

"The murder scene?" I said. "Or in the building where the murder scene occurred? That's two different things. I'm sure you know that."

The detective didn't appear to appreciate the correction, glaring back at me, eyes narrowed.

I said, "It was his girlfriend's apartment building. Just because he was there, doesn't mean—"

"Mr. Mason was present around the approximate time the murder had occurred," she said.

I didn't have a response.

She said, "So, you said his sister called you? She's the reason you came down here?"

I paused, still debating in my head how much more I should tell the police what I knew about Brock and Kathy. It wasn't much, but it still bothered me a little, considering they both trusted me.

More than I trusted either one of them, at least.

"She thought he was in trouble," I said. "As I did."

"But she knew he wasn't actually missing at all?"

"Obviously," I said, nodding. "He was afraid I wouldn't help him clear his name."

"You seem to think he didn't kill her, but—"

"I don't see you have the kind of evidence you'd need to convict someone just for being caught on camera being inside his girlfriend's building."

She waited, as if wondering how to follow up. She might've been a detective, but I could tell she was working hard to cover up how raw she was.

Detective Collins looked at the papers in the folder again, took out a pen from the pocket on her suit jacket, and scribbled something on the inside flap of the folder. "So, you'd never met Jillian Rogers?"

I shook my head. "Never even heard the name before," I said. "I told you, it's been a dozen years since I saw Brock or Kathy."

She wrote something else with her pen. "Did he tell you why he thought she'd gone all the way up to Jacksonville?"

"I already answered questions," I said. "Aren't they written down somewhere? He told me someone called him from a private number. Everything he told me, if he's telling the truth—and that may be up for debate—it sounds to me like there's a good chance someone set him up."

The detective gazed into the distance, pulling her chin. "Did he tell you the last time he spoke to Jillian?"

I had to think about it. "I don't remember if he did or didn't."

"And you don't find it odd, he talks to you, makes the six-and-a-half-hour drive to Miami that same night?"

"It's five and a half," I said.

She gave me a look, like she didn't appreciate the specifics.

"I'm just saying, every minute counts, right? Considering the time of death—"

"Do you really believe what you're saying? Or are you just trying to protect your friend?" she said.

"I already told you some things he wouldn't want you to know. But that doesn't mean I'll sit back while he gets dragged down for a murder he may not've committed."

"But he might have," she said, a smirk-like grin on her face.

I thought about it some more, looking at the camera on the wall pointing toward me. I nodded toward it. "Is this conversation being recorded?"

She glanced over her shoulder toward the camera and nodded as she turned back.

There were a few seconds of silence between us, the detective with her eyes back on the folder with the papers. "His sister isn't talking," she said.

"She isn't talking?" I said, my first thought the cause of it being the accident and the injuries she must have sustained. "How bad is she?"

Detective Collins shook her head. "Oh, I'm sorry. I don't mean... She isn't talking, not because she can't. She wouldn't confirm anything you'd told us. The only thing she did say is she hadn't seen her brother in weeks. As for her condition, she's already been released from the hospital. Minor injuries."

I was relieved, and at the same time not completely surprised she wasn't going to rat out her brother the way I had.

I looked my hands over, with cuts and scrapes from the accident. "I think it should be explained to her that it's in her best interest to come clean," I said. "For the sake of Brock's life. Doesn't she realize these men that were after us, were likely the same ones who were parked outside that motel?"

"Like I said, she wouldn't talk," the detective said. "And, don't take this the wrong way, Mr. Walsh, but I don't need you to tell me how to do my job."

I wasn't sure I had. "I didn't know I did."

The detective grinned, the line between her lips straight and tight. She stood from the chair. "Until we find Brock Mason, I'm not sure what to believe right now."

"You think I'm lying?" I said.

"I didn't say that. But he wasn't at that motel, as I've already told you. The only proof of anything we have right now is that you drove recklessly on a public freeway. Until we have some kind of proof anything else you've told is true, then—"

"So you *don't* believe me," I said. "You think I made it all up? For what?"

"There is no proof or evidence, at the present time," she said. "Again, I'm not saying I think you're lying. But we have yet to find any proof of another vehicle that may have caused your accident. And you told us Mr. Mason was at a motel where we found no sign of him whatsoever. There's no record of his stay."

"You think he'd register under his own name?" I said, shaking my head. "Of course he wouldn't."

The young detective eyebrows were knitted tight. She started to say something, then stopped, and turned for the door.

"You're free to go," she said, opening the door.

"That's it?" I said, unsure why the so-called interview with the detective turned out to be nothing.

"We have your statement," she said.

"Isn't there anything else you need from me? I'd like to help however I—"

The young detective put her hand up to me and pulled her phone off of her belt. She gave it a look, and whatever expression she had on her face was gone. "I'm sorry, please wait right here a moment." She left the room and closed the door behind her.

I sat in silence, but could hear her voice outside the door.

I looked at my watch. Without my phone, I couldn't even reach out to Alex to let her know how things had turned. It was a disaster, it seemed. I should have listened to her, and stayed home.

As usual, it was looking like she turned out to be right.

The door opened and Detective Collins came into the room. She looked like she was about to speak, but stopped herself, cleared her throat, and closed the door behind her.

"Brock Mason's body was found in a parking lot, off Northwest Ninth, two blocks from the motel where you said you last saw him."

Chapter 11

WITHOUT A CAR AND with a cell phone that was dead, I had no choice but to take Detective Collins up on her offer to drive me back to the hotel. And on the ride over, she seemed to have more questions than she did the whole time I was at the station. A lot of her questions were more personal, most having to do with my work as a private investigator.

She pulled up to the front entrance to the hotel and put her Chevy Impala in park. "It sounds like you're a good detective," she said. "But if you don't mind, I'm going to ask you to stay out of our way from this point forward. I know he was your friend, or whatever you want to call him, but right now..."

"I'm sorry," I said. "But I'm allowed to investigate. You can't really tell me not to."

She smiled, as if humored by my suggestion she didn't have the power or authority to tell me to stay out of the way. "I know I can't demand you step away," she said. "But, let me put it another way..." She looked straight ahead, her gaze toward her headlights shining on the gated pool area that was practically dropped in the middle of the parking lot. "I think it would be in your best interest. I don't think we need to be bumping heads. And, you have to admit, your past relationship with Brock and his sister certainly makes me feel you're going to be a bit more biased, than—"

"I told you everything I knew," I said. "I would hardly call it going out of my way to help him. I would say it's quite the opposite, wouldn't you?"

The detective turned to me, staring without another word as I stepped out from the passenger seat. "Be safe, Mr. Walsh," she said, waiting for me to close the door, without another word.

I backed from her maroon Chevy Impala and watched her race across the parking lot, her tires skidding as she turned onto the street.

·····•·•····

The first thing I did after I checked in and got into my room was plug my phone into the outlet over the nightstand. I sat on the edge of the bed and watched the phone power on, then laid back with my head on the pillow and looked up at the ceiling for a few minutes. I needed to gather my broken thoughts, and hadn't really had a chance to try and pull everything together.

It was hard to believe Brock was dead, although far from unbelievable. Especially considering I'd come down to Miami with the belief he'd already been dead.

Once the phone had finally cycled through the long startup process, I entered my password and watched one notification after another pop up on the screen. I had at least nineteen text messages and four voicemails. A few of the texts were from Billy, and just about every other one from Alex, on top of the four voicemails she'd left me.

But there was one other call that had come in from a 305 area code.

Of course, I called Alex back right away, and she answered on the first ring, with panic in her voice: "Henry? Where are you? Are you all right? I called the Miami-Dade police, but they wouldn't tell me anything, other than you'd been in an accident."

"That's all they told you?" I said. "I'm fine. I'm all right. I just checked into the hotel five minutes ago."

"But why didn't you call me? I've been texting. I called you, I don't know how many times..."

"The police took my phone. And by the time I got it back, the battery was dead. I'm sorry."

"You couldn't have called me from the police station?"

She was right. I apologized again, then told her most of what had happened throughout the past ten or so hours.

"So, Brock lied to you, made you think he was dead? You get down there, and somebody kills him? Nobody knows anything else?"

"I don't know what the police know. I don't think the detective's interested in sharing anything with me."

"And Brock's sister lied about the whole thing?"

"According to the detective. But I haven't talked to Kathy."

"Are you going to call her?"

I wasn't prepared for Alex's questions. Or, the truth was, I was too tired to answer all of them. My brain wasn't in a place to be able to keep up with hers. My body was weak. I was tired.

I glanced at the number on my phone with the 305 area code. "I told you, my phone's been dead. I'll call her when we get off."

There was silence on the line.

"Are you okay?" Alex said.

I had to think about it. "I guess so."

"You *guess* so?"

"I'm fine. I need to eat. I need to sleep." I smelled my shirt. "And I could certainly use a shower." It was right then I realized I didn't have my bag. "Oh no."

"What's wrong?" Alex said.

"I don't have any clothes to change into. I left my duffel bag in the trunk of the detective's car." I pulled out my wallet for the card with her number, then glanced out the window at the shopping center across the street from the hotel.

Alex said, "Can't you call him?"

"Her," I said. "But, I guess I should call her. Kind of strange, she's driving around with my clothes in the trunk of her car." I looked at my watch, even though I already knew it was late.

"Are you sure you're all right down there?" she said. "If you need me to, I can come down. You don't even have a car."

"I know," I said. "I also have to get Billy's car repaired. I have no idea what it'll cost."

"That's what insurance is for," she said.

"One more accident and they're going to drop me," I said. "You know how it works. Insurance companies are great until you need them." I thought about Billy. "I haven't even called Billy yet. He's not going to be happy."

We both paused on the line.

"You don't need to come down here," I said. "I'm fine."

"You don't sound fine," Alex said. "My parents will understand if I have to help you."

"No, that's foolish," I said.

"I don't think it is."

We were both silent again.

"Let me call you back," I said. "I'll figure out what I'm going to do once I get something in my stomach."

I was by no means dressed for a night out, but it wasn't that bad, either. As long as someone didn't get stuck somehow sitting too close to me.

I got off the phone with Alex and promised her a call when I got back to the hotel. And she made it clear I'd pay for it if she didn't hear from me within a reasonable amount of time.

I looked at the screen for the number with the 305 area code that had called my phone, then checked Kathy's number. But it wasn't hers, and I could only assume she would have called me with her cell phone if she was trying to reach me.

I tapped the phone number and sat on the edge of the bed, trying to ignore my growling stomach.

I stood from the bed and decided to leave the room, the phone to my ear as I stepped out into the hall. A younger woman was out there and walked right past me, her eyes down on her phone like she didn't even know I was there.

Sometimes saying hi to a stranger seemed like it had become a thing of the past, especially for the younger generation. On the other hand, a middle-aged guy like myself might've been creepy, in a younger person's eyes.

The phone rang two times on the other end, then stopped and went straight to voicemail. It was obvious when someone hit the ignore key rather than not being available to answer a call. The fact was, unless someone was asleep or dead, very few phone calls you made were actually missed anymore. Sadly, few people would, or could, go ten feet without a phone in their hand.

A message came on and stated there was no voicemail set up on the phone. Then the call ended.

I looked at my phone to make sure I'd done everything right on my end, then continued down the hall and stopped at the elevators. The woman who had walked past me in the hall was already waiting, but kept her eyes on her phone as if I wasn't right there next to her.

The elevator bell dinged and the woman glanced at me for the first time and actually smiled. I gestured for her to go ahead of me. And before I stepped on after her, my phone buzzed.

I had a message from the same number I'd called:

Don't call back. I will call you in one hour.

The woman was on the elevator waiting for me.

"Sorry," I said. "Go ahead."

Before she could even respond, the elevator door slid closed and she didn't bother trying to stop it.

I stood in the hallway and responded to the text:

Who is this?

I waited, tapped the button for the elevator to go down, and looked at my phone.

Whoever it was didn't respond.

Chapter 12

I WAS SURPRISED TO see the bar at the Mexican place I went into, across from the hotel, as crowded as it was. I couldn't tell if Zapata's was a chain or not, but guessed the free chips and the lime-green margarita slush churning in the machine on the far end of the bar was the likely attraction. The sign on the machine read, "$3 Margaritas!"

I wasn't sure why I chose to eat Mexican. Some people were smarter than me, and turned their nose up at a specific food or drink from a previous bad experience. But, for me, when I'm as hungry as I was, my mind seemed to forget unpleasant meals from my past.

It's not that I'd ever had a specific, life-altering issue eating Mexican food. But it's the kind that always started off as the best-tasting meal I'd ever had, and I'd dig into it hard, as if it was my first bite of food in weeks. But then I'd get halfway through the meal—whether it was a burrito or some kind of dish I couldn't properly pronounce—and it started to be, well, not quite as good once it began to settle in my stomach.

Without fail, by the time the plate was cleaned off, I wished I'd ordered a salad.

But I'd never been one to learn my lessons.

I polished off the basket of free tortilla chips before I'd even ordered, then bellied up to a bean burrito that practically hung off both sides of the long, oval plate.

I finished just over half of the burrito, and even though I'd gone with the veggie version, I was starting to hit that point where I knew I'd made a mistake.

I ordered an iced tea to wash it all down.

Seated on the side of the bar closest to the door, there was an empty stool to my left and right; every other stool along the bar was occupied. And just about every person, minus one or two, looked to be drinking that lime-green margarita slush in a tall margarita glass.

It'd been at least a year since I'd had a drink, give or take a month or two. And I'd gotten well past the point of being tempted to crack a bottle anytime I sat at a bar. I no longer watched everyone around me with some kind of envy because they seemed to be having a better time than me.

I wiped my hands with the cloth napkin and thought about calling it quits on the burrito before it turned to regret.

I'd been staring at my phone, waiting for it to ring, but hadn't gotten the call I was promised in the text. Part of me believed it was Kathy who had sent the text, but I couldn't come up with a good enough reason for why she wouldn't be able to talk. Or why she wouldn't have left a message.

It also didn't make sense the text had come from a different number, unless Kathy was, for some reason, hiding calls from her husband.

I checked the time of the text, and it was getting close to being almost exactly one hour since I'd received it.

The bartender came over. He was a middle-aged white dude with a mustache and a bit of a belly, and asked if everything was all right.

I pushed the plate with the half-eaten burrito toward him. "I'm good," I said. I felt dehydrated, and the salt-soaked burrito didn't help.

I ordered a glass of water and it had a strong, chlorine-like flavor, which made me feel worse than I had without it.

"You want to take it home?" he said, lifting the messy plate.

"I'd better not," I said, and smiled. I imagined the clothes I was wearing; the sweat dried into the threads would be bad enough sitting on the floor of the hotel room. I didn't need the place reeking of leftover Mexican food.

The bartender disappeared through the swinging door with my plate.

I flipped through my phone to see what else I could dig up about Brock, wondering if there'd been any leads on the case, or if it'd even made it into the news. I was somewhat surprised to find nothing at all about Brock, other than the old article Alex had already dug up.

The bartender came back through the swinging door and stopped and stood in front of me. "You on vacation?"

"Not exactly," I said.

"Work?"

"You could say that." I wasn't about to go into any details.

He turned and glanced to his left at the other patrons seated along the bar, then leaned into me. "You a cop?"

I held back a grin. It had been a while since anyone had asked me that. "Do I look like one?"

He shrugged, then nodded. "My cousin's a cop up in Orlando. You got the same look, that's all."

"What look is that?"

He shrugged. "I don't know. Just a look, I guess."

I still had my phone in my hand, but placed it facedown on the bar. "Can I get the check?"

The guy made a face like he didn't appreciate my lack of interest in having any kind of conversation. He stepped away toward the back of the bar, tapped a button on the computer and printed out my slip. He tucked it under the salt shaker. "Whenever you're ready."

I looked at my phone again and saw that it'd been over an hour now since I'd received the text. Six minutes past an hour, to be exact. I put my credit card on the bar by my check without looking at it and waited for the bartender to come back over.

My phone buzzed, and I answered right away.

"Hello?" I said, my voice somewhat hushed. I didn't like being the guy at the bar talking on his phone. But I wasn't going to risk missing the call.

"Is this Henry Walsh?" the male caller said.

"Who's asking?" I said.

There was a pause. "My name's Steve. Steve Rogers." His voice was also somewhat hushed.

"Rogers?" It took me less than a second to make the connection. "Any relation to Jillian Rogers?"

"Well, sort of," he said.

The bartender took my credit card and I watched him slide it through the card machine.

"You're her husband?" I said. "I didn't realize she—"

"Ex-husband," he said.

"Oh." I grabbed my credit card from the bartender, gave him a nod, and headed for the door.

"It's been a long time since we were married," he said. "We'd known each other since we were kids."

It was dark out, and I started across the well-lit parking lot, heading back toward the hotel across the street. The smell of coffee hung in the air, and I thought I could use some caffeine.

"Can I ask how you got my name? And this number?" I said. "And why you had to play games, calling me the way you did?"

"I'll tell you more when we meet," he said. "And, well, I have to be careful."

"When we meet?" I said. I started walking toward a coffee shop I spotted, a place called The Coffee Bean. How original. But it looked busy enough inside, where I could see the small crowd clearly through the all-glass storefront, the place brightly lit inside.

"So, you want to meet?" I said.

"I'd like to. Tonight, if possible."

"Tonight?" I looked at my watch, turning so I could catch the glow from one of the streetlights to see better. It was nine thirty.

"I think it would be best," he said. "I know you were a friend of Brock Mason's."

"You knew him?" I said.

"You could say that. To be honest, it's not a surprise what happened to her, getting caught up with someone like him."

"What's that supposed to mean?" I said, as if surprised, even though I knew exactly what he meant.

He didn't elaborate. "So, you're a private investigator, huh? From Jacksonville? I got a cousin up that way. Haven't talked to him in a long time though. Not even sure he's still there."

I stood outside the entrance to the coffee shop and looked up at the sign. I said, "I'm at a place called the Coffee Bean, in the plaza across from the hotel where I'm staying."

"Coffee?" he said. "I can't drink caffeine this late. I'm actually heading out for a drink. Wife's at her book club, or whatever she's doing. I don't ask. But it's my night to get out. There's a place off Biscayne Boulevard, right on the bay. Can you meet me there?"

I, of course, didn't even have any wheels. And I wasn't exactly up for hopping in a cab unless this guy was willing to give me a good enough reason for meeting him.

"How about we meet somewhere in the morning? I'm not even sure how far I am from... What's the name of the place?"

"Mickey Cho's Water Club. Nice place, next to the Hilton Hotel. Got good Sushi, if you're hungry."

The last thing I wanted by then was something else in my stomach. I could still taste the burrito, and had a feeling in my gut like I'd swallowed a bag of cement.

I glanced at my watch again, as if I'd forgotten what time it was from thirty seconds earlier. "All right," I said, looking toward a men's clothing store with lights on. "I'm going to need some time. Maybe a half hour, forty-five minutes."

"Yeah, of course," Steve said. "I'll be at the bar."

Chapter 13

IT CROSSED MY MIND to use one of those new driver services I could order if I felt like putting another app on my phone. But there was something about getting in the back seat of a car driven by a guy who'd likely been in the middle of a video game when he decided to become a pro driver.

Maybe it wasn't like that at all, but when I'd gotten back to the hotel for some new clothes to change into, a cab was parked outside my hotel.

I walked up to the cab's driver side, and the driver rolled down the window, giving me a nod with his chin. "You need a ride?"

"Can you take me to a place called Mickey Cho's, off Biscayne?" I'd forgotten the specific street address Rogers had given me.

"Get in," the cabbie said.

"I need to go up to my room. Can you give me a few minutes?"

Cabbie shrugged, nodding. "Take all the time you need. Meter's running."

I hurried through the front entrance to the hotel and across the lobby for the elevators, pressing the up button.

I waited, pulling out my phone to call Alex.

The phone rang three or four times before she finally answered.

"Hey," I said. "I just got a call from this guy, Steve Rogers. Get this: He's the ex-husband of Jillian Rogers."

"Her ex-husband? He called you?" she said. "What about?"

"Well, he didn't say. But I'm meeting him at some bar. Or, I guess it's a restaurant."

"I thought you went out to eat earlier?" she said.

"I did."

The bell dinged on the elevator and the door slid open.

Alex said, "So he didn't say what he wanted?"

I was happy to see the elevator empty when I stepped inside. "Of course, it's got to do with Jillian and Brock. But no, he didn't give any details."

"Henry?" she said, and I could tell by her tone she was about to go into full-mom mode. "I don't think you should go."

"Why not? It's not like I'm meeting him down some dark alley. We'll be in a public place. And he sounded like a normal guy."

"You think you can tell? From a phone call?"

"I'm usually right," I said. "Minus the dozens of times I haven't been."

Alex didn't laugh. "Can't you just let the police handle it?"

"I could," I said. "But, I just don't think I have anything to lose. Besides, it's not like I can leave Miami until Billy's car's fixed anyway."

Alex said, "How long is that supposed to take?"

"I have no idea," I said. "But I'm not just going to sit around, twiddling my thumbs."

Alex let out a loud sigh, as if she wanted to make sure I heard it.

"I'll be fine," I said. "All right?"

"You have no idea who this guy is. And you have no idea what he wants."

"Did you at least look him up?" she said.

I hadn't.

"I was going to," I said. "But..."

The line went quiet again, and I could hear clicking coming through the phone.

"What are you doing?" I said.

"Looking him up. You said his name was Steve?"

"Steve Rogers."

The elevator stopped at the sixth floor and I stepped off, turning right, then looking at the sign straight ahead with the range of room numbers posted on it, with half the rooms to the right, the other half to the left. My room, number 6013, was to the right.

For one reason or another, I didn't remember which way I was supposed to go.

Alex said, "You sure this guy's last name is Rogers? I'm not finding anyone."

I slipped my key card into the door, tried the handle with the phone pressed between my ear and shoulder, but got nothing other than a red light that lit up on top of the lock.

Alex had said something else, but I didn't hear her, and asked her to hang on while I tried the door once again. This time, the green light on the lock turned on, but the handle wouldn't budge. I slid the key card into the lock again, got the green light and a click, and yanked the handle downward, driving my shoulder into the door. It opened with a pop, like I broke something on the lock. I just about stumbled into the room when it swung open.

Alex said, "What are you doing?"

"Nothing. Sorry. I couldn't get in my room."

"You can't get in?"

"No, it's okay. I'm in now."

There was another pause, until Alex said, "I don't like any of this."

I dumped the bag of clothes I'd just bought onto the bed. "Stop worrying," I said. "This guy tracked me down somehow. I don't even know how he knew about me. But, he obviously has something to tell me."

"Have you considered it could be some kind of a setup?" Alex said.

I looked at the red digits on the digital clock next to the king-size bed. It was getting late, and I was paying for the cab to wait for me. "Stop overthinking it," I said. "I gotta go."

She said, "Will you at least call me when you get there?"

"When I get there? How about when I'm done talking to the guy?"

It took her a moment to respond. "Henry, just make sure you don't leave me hanging again."

"Again?" I said, even though I knew what she meant. "I won't."

I got off the phone with Alex and changed into the new clothes, hurrying for the door. But just as I reached for the knob, my phone buzzed in my pocket.

It was a text from Kathy:

Are you all right?

I continued from the room and down the hall, thinking about my text before I replied. I thought about how she'd lied to the cops, but didn't think texting was the best way to discuss it.

I texted back:

I'm fine. Are you okay?

I pressed the button for the elevator and waited.

Kathy texted back:

We need to talk.

The elevator door opened and there was a woman and man standing there watching me. I stepped on, gave a nod to the couple, then answered the text:

When?

I rode the elevator down and into the lobby and Kathy had texted back as the door opened:

Luke knows about us.

I knew what she meant, but it honestly didn't make much sense. I wasn't sure why it mattered. I replied:

Knows what?

It's funny, Kathy and I hadn't really touched on the subject of our past relationship at all at any point, although it wasn't exactly relevant. It was history, and as far as I was concerned didn't make much of a difference.

The cab driver was luckily still waiting for me, parked outside the hotel. "I was afraid you weren't going to show up," he said, looking over his shoulder at me when I slid into the back seat.

"Sorry it took so long."

The cabbie picked up a New York Yankees cap and slipped it on his head. "Okay with me. I told you, meter's running."

He shifted into drive and took off toward the street. "You said you're going to Mickey Cho's?"

"You know where it is?" I said, my eyes on my phone's screen again, waiting for a text back from Kathy.

"Of course," the cab driver said.

My head snapped back when he slammed his foot on the gas, cutting in front of oncoming cars like they weren't there.

My phone buzzed. But this time it wasn't Kathy.

It was the alleged Steve Rogers, texting me to tell me he was at the bar waiting.

I texted him back:

On my way.

The cab driver had his radio on, in a language I didn't understand or recognize.

I hadn't heard back from Kathy by the time the cabbie turned into the Hilton Hotel, overlooking Biscayne Bay. Next to it was the freestanding restaurant, the bright, neon lighting on the front that read Mickey Cho's in big, script-like letters, with Water Club in smaller letters underneath.

The cabbie turned with his arm hung over the front seat's backrest. He held his hand out. "Thirty-three dollars," he said.

I tried to contain my surprise for what was a costly four-minute ride, but handed him my credit card.

"I told you, the meter was running," he said. He swiped it on a portable machine attached by a spiral cord to the dashboard, my card still stuck inside. "Sign please?"

I took the device, saw it already had the suggested tip included with my total. I signed my signature with the plastic pen and left it as it was. "Thanks," I said, stepping out of the cab.

I looked around the parking lot outside the restaurant, especially where the lot wasn't completely full. There were a couple of cars running with lights on toward the back of the lot, but I thought nothing of it.

I walked toward the entrance and checked my phone one more time. Kathy still hadn't texted back, and I wondered what had happened.

I wanted to ask her if she knew anything about Steve Rogers, before I went inside to meet him. So rather than send a text, I decided to call.

It rang once, and someone answered.

I said, "Kathy?"

A man's voice came through the other end. "Who the hell's this?"

All I could assume was it was her husband, Luke.

"Is Kathy around?" I said, without answering the man's question.

"You gonna answer me?" he said in a deeper southern drawl than I was expecting. I could picture him chewing a toothpick, straightening his John Deere hat, waiting for me to respond.

"This is Henry," I said. "But you probably know that. Can I talk to her?"

"She doesn't want to talk to you," he said.

And before I could respond, the call had ended.

I didn't want to upset the guy any more than he apparently already was.

I reached for the door handle at the entrance to Mickey Cho's.

But the door swung open and a man hurried through it, practically knocking me out of the way. He wore a dark baseball cap and sunglasses, which I found odd, considering it was dark out.

I watched him pick up his pace, until he broke into a run, hotfooting it out of the parking lot. A car pulled up on the street and he jumped inside.

Screams came from inside the restaurant, and as I again reached for the door handle, a crowd of people—women, men, and younger kids—came crashing through, all running from the restaurant.

I stayed out of the way, with no idea what I was witnessing or what had happened.

Of course, I knew the man who'd walked right past me had to've had something to do with it.

I slipped into the restaurant once the crowd had cleared and emptied into the parking lot. Car headlights came on and some people drove off while others seemed to hang around, watching the restaurant. I could hear a lot of crying, mostly from kids.

I took a few hurried steps through the area at the entrance and kicked something across the wood floor. Looking down, I saw a long, blood-covered knife.

I didn't pick it up, but continued ahead and through a doorway with double doors propped open. I walked into the bar area, where a man was slumped on a stool, the back of his light-colored dress shirt soaked in blood.

A man I assumed was the bartender stood on the other side, across the bar from him, phone up to his ear, talking to what sounded like the 9-1-1 operator from what I could hear. His skin was ghost-white, gaze toward me now, like he was in some kind of a trance.

There was another man, about my size and build, dressed in a Hawaiian shirt and khaki shorts. But he had his back to me, standing next to the old man slumped over the bar, the man leaning toward the slumping man, head turned as if trying to listen for something.

I stepped closer and looked at the slumping man's bloodied back.

"Is he dead?" I said.

The man in the Hawaiian shirt straightened up and turned to look at me. He shrugged. "I don't know."

I stepped forward and felt for the slumping man's pulse, then looked from the man in the Hawaiian shirt to the bartender, nodding. "Yeah, he's dead."

The bartender was off the phone now, and stuck a cigarette in his mouth. His hands were shaking, eyes wide open.

The man standing next to the body just stood there without a word.

"What happened?" I said. "Do either of you know who he is?"

Neither man answered, but they both looked at each other.

It was an odd scene, the way the three of us stood there as if none of us knew what to say while a dead guy slumped over the bar. The TV over the bar had a Miami Marlins game on, the sound turned off.

I could still hear people crying outside; one woman seemed to be screaming hysterically. Frank Sinatra's "Fly Me to the Moon" played over the speakers on the ceiling.

There was a smell of something grilling, perhaps burning, that seemed to get stronger.

Under the dead man's stool was a broken glass, whatever drink he had mixed in with the blood still dripping from above.

The place had mostly cleared out, other than the two men waiting with the body. I turned when I thought I saw someone, and a short man in all white and a cook's hat poked his head out from a swinging door. He had a fire extinguisher in his hand, yelled something in Spanish at us, then pulled his head back and disappeared.

Sirens screamed from somewhere in the distance, but grew louder.

The bartender, middle-aged I guessed, wore a white buttoned shirt with the sleeves rolled up and a black bow tie. He lit his cigarette. "I didn't see what happened." He looked at the man in the Hawaiian shirt, then at me. "There was no gunshot."

"He was stabbed," I said, nodding toward the hallway leading to the entrance. "There's a bloody knife out there, by the entrance."

I said to the bartender. "Do you know his name?"

He shook his head.

The man standing by the dead guy reached for a red-colored drink on the bar, then took a sip from a cocktail straw. He gave me a nod with his chin. "Who are you, exactly?"

"I was supposed to meet a man here. And I have a feeling that's him."

"You don't know?" the man said. "You want to get a better look?" He waved, gesturing for me to step closer to the body.

I glanced into the dining room, where it looked like dishes were smashed on the floor, half the chairs knocked over.

I said, "I was supposed to meet someone here. But I'd never met the guy before, so..."

The man sipped what was left of his red drink and pushed the empty glass toward the bartender on the other side. "Ricky, get me one more before the cops show up, will you?"

The sirens were louder now, blue and red lights coming through the windows and reflecting off the restaurant's white walls.

I said to the bartender, "Did he say anything at all to you?"

The bartender shrugged. "Not really. Might've mentioned something about a night off, his wife at her book club."

Chapter 14

THERE WERE AT LEAST a dozen police officers from both the City of Miami Police and the Miami-Dade Police Department. In addition to a couple of rescue vehicles and a fire truck, there were two news vans parked in the restaurant's parking lot, where most of the cars had been cleared.

It was hard to say whether or not this was some kind of hit job. The cop who questioned me wasn't ready to call it that. I'd witnessed one myself, back when I was a trooper up in Rhode Island, where a man they called "Joe the Barber" was the victim of a mob hit while seated at a bar on Federal Hill. It had the same feel.

But I did my best to describe the man I saw leaving the bar to the cop who questioned me.

I was on the phone with Alex, giving her a brief rundown of what had happened, when I noticed the man from inside the bar, the one with the red drink, talking to a couple of police officers.

He turned to look my way, as if he knew I was watching him, then said something else to the cops before starting toward me. "I hear you're a private investigator?" he said.

I nodded, watching him approach me. "What about you?"

"What about me?" he said.

"You a cop?"

The man cracked a grin, like I'd said something funny. "No."

"I didn't think so," I said. "I figured you would've stopped what'd happened in there, if you were."

"Oh, if I could've, I... I was actually in the head when it happened." The man reached out and shook my head. "Joe Sheldon."

"Henry Walsh."

"I know," Joe said.

I glanced over at the police officers Joe had been talking to. I said, "You seem to be in with them?"

"In?" he said. "With who, the cops?" Joe shrugged, nodding. "I was a journalist in my past life. Covered crime for the *Miami Post*."

"Yeah?" I said. "No more?"

"Forced retirement."

I thought about my own forced retirement, although I hoped Joe's was under better circumstances. Glancing toward the restaurant's entrance, I said, "I wonder what the word is in there."

Joe looked at his watch. "I've been coming to this place for a while. Never thought I'd see something like this. Although it is Miami," he said.

The bagged body was finally rolled outside on the gurney. I wasn't sure how much I should say to Joe, or if he was even up for discussing what we'd both seen. I said, "So, what do you do now? You still write?"

Joe had a look like he didn't want to answer, pausing a moment. "I'm working on a book."

"Yeah?" I was impressed, although I knew a lot of people claimed the same thing, knowing the chances they'd ever finish were slim. It was no different than runners you see out there in January who run for a few weeks, then quit. Or someone who buys all the paint supplies, but never puts the brush to the canvas...

Joe said, "I do some side work too, for an old friend."

"What kind of work?" I said.

He pulled the toothpick from his mouth. "I guess you could call it investigative work. I'm not licensed as a PI or anything, but..." He looked around, kept his voice low. "The guy I work for isn't the straightest cat around, if you know what I mean?"

I decided not to ask for details. He seemed like a decent enough guy, but maybe the type who could go either way, when it came to the law.

"I imagine you know a lot of people around here?" I said.

"Here?" he said, pointing at the ground. "Miami?"

"Yeah, sure. Miami. Florida. As someone who covered crime, you must—"

"You have a specific question in mind?" he said.

I looked around to make sure there weren't any cops nearby. "That guy in there. I was supposed to meet him about something that, well... I have an old acquaintance, name's Brock Mason, I was just wondering if you—"

"Mason?" he said. He pulled at his chin. "Is he the one who worked for Raymond Canzano? Did time for some kind of employment scheme, something that had to do with ex-cons, right?"

I nodded. "What else do you know about it?"

"Not much," Joe said. "It's just that, well, Ray Canzano's got a reputation around Miami, so…"

"What kind of reputation?" I said.

"Rumor was always that he had connections."

"Like what? You mean—"

"The Mob," Joe said. "New York guy, so everyone just assumes…"

"But you have no proof of it?" I said. "That he's connected?"

Sheldon shook his head. "Never been any real evidence of it, no. I can't speak for the Feds or anything like that, but… Are you saying what happened in there had something to do with your buddy? Or Canzano?"

"I don't know. He—Brock Mason—was mixed up in something. Not to mention, a suspect in a murder. Of course, he claimed he didn't do it. But somebody tried to make it look like he did." I glanced toward a couple of officers who seemed to be talking while both looking our way. I kept my voice low. "You mentioned Canzano. You think I should talk to him?" I looked at the coroner's van, the bright, white backup lights illuminating the area behind it.

Joe shrugged. "You're asking the wrong guy. I'm not even sure what you want to talk to him about. Mason's dead girlfriend?"

"Well, about everything."

Joe had a confused look on his face, like he didn't understand. "So, where is he now?" Joe said.

"Who?"

"Brock Mason."

"Oh, Brock's dead."

Joe smiled. "Now I get it. I think I missed that important piece of information."

"I don't remember the last time I slept," I said.

We both huffed out a slight laugh.

I said, "So were you involved in the reporting, with this scheme Brock was busted for?"

Joe shook his head. "Not directly. Buddy of mine, Mac Sullivan." He looked toward the ground. "Sully was a good guy, killed in a car wreck a few years back."

"Yeah?"

Joe nodded. "Taught me a lot. We were both let go from the paper within the same year."

"You don't think his accident had anything to do with the kind of work you guys did, do you?"

Joe paused, like he was thinking about it. "I like to think the answer to that is no. Otherwise, I'd never sleep." He pulled another toothpick from his pocket and stuck it between his teeth. Joe kept his voice hushed. "So, how much of this did you share with the cops?"

"About Brock?"

Joe shrugged. "I don't know. All of it, I guess."

"They're involved already. I've been questioned, probably told them more than I should have. But I don't know if I'd say they're interested in me being involved at this point." The coroner's van drove past us and toward the street. "I was hoping that man in there was going to shed some light on a few things. I guess that ship has sailed."

"The one who was stabbed? Rogers?"

I nodded. "He was married to Brock Mason's girlfriend."

"The dead one?"

"Yeah. She still used his last name," I said.

"Oh, okay. Jillian Rogers. Steve Rogers." He ran his hand down his face. "This one's a little sticky," he said. "So, the ex-husband and Mason's girlfriend were still hanging around together?"

"I don't know the details of their relationship. I guess I would've found out. But somebody saw to it he wouldn't have the chance to open his mouth."

"Who's the detective on the case?" Joe said. "I know most of them."

"Her name's Mia Collins," I said. "She's young. In her twenties, I'd say."

"Miami-Dade PD?" Joe said.

I nodded, and Joe shook his head. He said, "I'm not familiar with the name. The ones I know are older or retired. These young kids, different breed. I can see why you might not get along. They think us old guys are all idiots, too far behind the times with all this technology they have today."

Joe and I both stood silent for a couple of moments.

I said, "So, what happened at the *Miami Post*? They forced you out?"

"I took a buyout. I still get paid a little. It's not as bad as being fired... just a way they can get us middle-aged guys out of there without any kind of age discrimination suits, you know?" He laughed.

"You don't look old enough to have to worry about age discrimination," I said.

"You'd be surprised. We might not think we're old. But someone else might. Some hotshot punk comes in, fresh out of an ivy league school, thinks she knows a thing or two..."

Joe looked off toward the water behind the restaurant. "It's not like it used to be, back when you'd work for the paper for forty-something years, retire with a big party and the gold watch. They want the kids now. Cheap labor's where it's at. All they gotta do is regurgitate the stuff someone else wrote, make sure it ends up good enough, get it up online and move on to the next hot topic. It's a race to the bottom, the news media today. Especially the newspapers... I don't know how they'll survive. I mean, most are already dead. Or close to it." He looked me over. "You remember how important the newspaper was when we were growing up? You had the newspaper, some magazines, the nightly news. They had to get it right. But most people are too lazy now, just scan the headlines on their phone, share it with their friends to make it look like they know a thing or two. You wonder why we're all getting dumber by the day."

I got the feeling Joe Sheldon had some resentment after losing his job. But I knew exactly where he was coming from.

"You ever think about doing something on your own? Maybe a blog? Or a podcast," I said. "I hear that's where it's at now. People are all into this true-crime stuff."

Joe huffed out a laugh, shaking his head. "Everyone's got a podcast now. Jesus. I got a buddy, lives in my building. He quit his tech job and that's all he does now. At least I think that's what he does. I don't know. Maybe he's on TikTok. Good guy, but I swear, nobody wants to do any real work anymore."

One of the police officers called out for Joe, and Joe waved back, gesturing that he'd be right over. He reached out and shook my hand. "Hey, good talking to you, man. Good luck with everything." He started to walk away.

I said, "Joe?"

He turned and I handed him my business card. "You happen to hear anything about what we talked about, or something else you might be able to share with me..."

He looked at my card, nodding, then pulled out a wallet from his front pocket and slipped the card inside. "Yeah, of course. Sure thing." He paused. "Oh, and sorry about your friend."

Chapter 15

It was well past midnight by the time I walked into my room at the hotel. When I spoke to Alex outside the restaurant, I'd promised her I'd call as soon as I got back. But before I had a chance to pick up the phone, someone knocked on my door.

I looked through the peephole.

Detective Mia Collins stood in the hall, and when I opened the door she reached out to me, holding my duffel bag. "You forgot something," she said.

I held off inviting her in.

"Is this business?" I said, then regretted the words the moment they left my mouth. "I'm sorry, I mean... Does this have to do with what happened tonight? Or..."

My phone rang from inside the room, and I accidentally let the door close when I turned to answer it, leaving the detective out in the hall.

I grabbed my phone and saw it was Alex, then hurried back to open the door. "Sorry about that," I said, then answered my phone. "Alex?"

She sounded annoyed. "Are you at the hotel?"

"Yeah, just walked in."

"Are you doing this on purpose?" Alex said.

"Doing *what* on purpose?" I kept my voice somewhat hushed, as if Detective Collins wouldn't hear me from just across the room, where she stood inside the closed door.

Alex said, "You keep telling me not to worry, but you keep leaving me hanging. You said you'd be back at the hotel a half hour ago."

"Yeah, I know. I'm sorry. But I'm here now. Only thing is, there's somebody here I need to—"

"Somebody's in your room?" she said.

"Oh, sorry. Detective Collins."

The detective was looking at her phone, but raised her gaze when I said her name.

"I'll let you go," Alex said. "But can you call me when she leaves? I can't stand this anymore. I wish you'd listened to me and stayed away."

"It's too late for that," I said. "I'll call you back." I hung up and turned to the detective. "Sorry about that."

She took a few more steps into the room. "I wasn't able to get a clear answer from the officers on duty at that restaurant. I don't understand exactly what you were doing there."

She hadn't gotten a clear answer because I did my best to avoid giving one, although I wasn't sure how much I had to hide.

She put her hands on her hips, moving the hem of her jacket enough so I could see her badge on the belt of her jeans with her holster on the opposite hip. "You claim you were there for a drink?" She folded her arms, eyes somewhat squinted. "Why Mickey Cho's? Weren't you already out tonight? Right across the street?"

I was surprised to hear she knew I'd gone out earlier. "You were watching me?" I said.

The detective cleared her throat, but I had a feeling she did it on purpose, as if to let me know I'd better not continue with the lies. "Well, let's just say we were keeping an eye out," she said. "For your own good."

"My own good?" I said. "So you already knew I went to Mickey Cho's?"

She shook her head. "I wish we had, then maybe this could have been avoided."

I had to think about what she was saying, and wondered how much more she knew than she was letting on.

I remembered the pile of clothes I left on the bathroom floor, and wondered what the inside of the room actually smelled like to the detective. I wasn't at all comfortable having her come any further into the room.

I said, "Do you mind if we get out of here? Maybe go downstairs, so we can talk? I'll tell you what I can."

"I want you to tell me the truth," she said.

I nodded. "Of course."

She turned and reached for the door. "Is there a bar?"

"No," I said.

I followed her out the door, the detective walking ahead of me but looking back as I pulled the door closed and made sure it was locked.

I picked up my pace to catch up to her. "The man who was killed," I said. "He knows Jillian Rogers. He's her ex-husband."

She glanced back at me. "We're aware of that," she said. "That's why this one's been turned over to me. Clearly, there's a connection between both homicides."

"Clearly," I said, walking side by side with her toward the elevator.

She said, "So why'd you lie to the officer? It doesn't look good." She acted as if she was trying to throw me a rope, before I got myself in any more trouble.

"I didn't want to get dragged down to the station again, as if I had something to do with this guy being stabbed."

We turned down the hall and stopped at the elevators.

She crossed her arms, eyes on the arrows above the elevator door. "Why should we believe you didn't have something to do with it?"

I said, "Because I wasn't there when it happened. There were witnesses. I showed up, the guy was dead."

The elevator door opened right away, with nobody else around.

"I'd like to say I believe you," she said. "But there are too many questions. Some things don't make much sense."

"You mean, that I had something to do with this man's death?" I said. "That's ridiculous."

"Is it?" she said, stepping into the elevator. She turned and leaned against the back wall, watching me as I walked in after her.

I waited for her to say more, but she remained silent, her eyes on the lighted numbers on the panel to the left of the elevator door.

"I told you I'll do whatever I can to help," I said.

She said, "I think being honest about your involvement, going back to your relationship with Brock Mason, would be a good start."

"There was no involvement," I said. "I already told you that. He was an old friend. An acquaintance, really. And it's not like he was ever up front with me about anything along the way. I've been as much in the dark as anybody."

The door opened and I waited for her to step out ahead of me into what appeared to be an empty lobby. There was nobody behind the desk.

I glanced over at a small seating area toward the hotel's entrance, surrounded and somewhat enclosed by large plants I believed might've been plastic. A large TV hung on the wall, with a red leather couch and three chairs facing each other.

"Do you want to sit there?" I said, pointing at the couch and chairs.

"Let's go outside," she said, sniffing. "I can't stand the smell of a hotel."

I wasn't exactly sure what she meant. Maybe it was the artificially scented air, or the overly familiar hotel smell, especially in the cheap chains, like the one I was staying in.

Detective Collins started for the door and walked outside.

It had cooled a bit since I'd gotten dropped off by the cab not even a half hour earlier. It was quiet around the hotel's parking lot, although cars buzzed by on the street to erase any silence. In fact, the sound was almost excessive, the way so many cars seemed to be souped-up nowadays to sound like race cars.

"Why is that legal?" I said.

The detective gave me a look, like she had no idea what I was talking about.

"The cars," I said. "These street racers. They're everywhere you go now, once the sun goes down... They take over the streets."

"Street takeovers," she said. "We've been trying to stop it, but—"

"Not even that. How do these cars pass inspection, the way they've got their mufflers making all that noise. My fiancée's poor dog, he won't even walk at night, these cars racing around, sometimes it sounds like gunshots coming out of their tailpipes."

Collins nodded, like she understood. But she didn't seem too interested in what might have come across as a diversion from the topic at hand.

She said, "Is that who you were talking to? Back there, in your room? Your fiancée."

I wasn't sure why it was any of her business, but nodded. I preferred not to pull Alex into any of it.

The detective had a smile on her face. "Is she in Jacksonville?"

"Well, we actually live in Fernandina Beach. We do have an office in Jacksonville, but... She's in Virginia, visiting her parents."

"You don't work alone?" she said, looking me over. "I picture you to be one of those lone wolves, likes to keep everything to himself, doesn't believe anyone else knows anything."

"Alex is my business partner," I said.

"Alex? I always liked that name. I had a doll when I was a little girl. Alexandria. I assume that's her full name?"

I hesitated, the detective somewhat prying into my personal business. "She's not involved in this at all," I said. "In fact, I'm tempted to get out of here myself."

"You're leaving Miami?"

"I'm thinking about it."

The detective shifted her gaze to the street. "I just hope you're going to be able to answer whatever questions we have."

"Isn't that why you're here?" I said. "I told you, I'll tell you what I know. But you're sending me mixed messages. Either you want my help, or you don't want my help."

She said, "Another homicide, one where you were present, has raised some eyebrows."

"I told you, he was dead when I got there."

"But from what it sounds like to me, you weren't exactly straight with the officers at the scene about why you were there."

"Maybe I just wasn't clear," I said.

Collins was quiet, as if thinking it all through. She said, "Have you communicated with Kathy Arnold?"

"Not since the accident," I said, knowing there was a chance she might already know I was lying. "Why are you coming after me and Kathy?" I said. "What about whoever practically killed us on that causeway?"

"Oh, I thought you already knew... We found the car," she said. "It was unregistered, with stolen plates. The vehicle was wiped clean of fingerprints or any kind of evidence."

"And you're sure it was the same car?"

She had her hands on her hips. "I don't like the way you question me."

I put my hands up. "I'm just trying to help."

Mia Collins took her phone from her pocket and looked at the glowing screen. She kept a neutral, calm look on her face. "I'm sorry," she said, and started across the parking lot. "We'll have to continue this conversation later." Her walk turned to a light jog, rushing to her vehicle, where she stepped into the driver's side and started the engine. She took off across the lot without another word, or ever looking back.

Chapter 16

A SLIVER OF SUNLIGHT slipped between the curtains and cut through the darkness in my hotel room. I'd been in bed for a handful of hours, dozing off here and there but not really getting much rest. On top of that, my mind was going in five different directions, the room's air-conditioning unit turned on and off every three minutes throughout the night. As much as I needed it, sleep wasn't going to be an option.

It took me a minute to find my phone, which I'd meant to charge but hadn't. I plugged it in while I got dressed, hoping I could get it enough juice to get me through the morning.

I was dressed and down in the lobby in time for the so-called breakfast they told me about, which turned out to be gas-station-quality muffins or bagels shipped in from some corporate distribution center across the country. There were only a handful of people down there, one being a man who looked like he'd had a few good meals in his lifetime, three plates in front of him with enough muffins to feed a family.

I did all I could to drink the coffee to get some caffeine into my blood, but couldn't quite get over the taste, tossing it into the trash on my way across the lobby.

The entrance doors slid open and my phone in my pocket buzzed.

When I pulled it out and looked at the screen, I saw Kathy had called, but hung up after a couple of rings before I answered.

I tapped her number and called right back.

Kathy answered right away, but spoke in a whisper. "Henry? I have to call you back. Where are you?"

"I'm at the hotel," I said. "Is everything all right? I mean... considering the circumstances?"

She paused. "We need to talk," she said. "But not right now. Can you meet me?"

"Well, I don't have a car. Unless you can swing by the hotel?"

"I can't," she said.

"You can't come to the hotel?"

"No," she said, and didn't offer a specific reason why. "Can't you take a cab?"

"Tell me where you want to meet," I said, looking back and forth for an option for transportation. There was a shuttle parked down the far end of the parking lot. "I'll be there."

She whispered. "Do you know where Sewell Park is?"

"Sewell Park? No idea. Is it near where I'm staying?" I wasn't sure if she even knew where my hotel was.

But she answered: "You can probably walk there."

I placed the call on speaker so I could type the name of it into my phone. The map showed it being a half hour, if I walked. I looked up at the bright sun, already heating up for the day. "I'll see you there."

"Meet me by the river," she said.

"What river?" I said, although I guessed it would be obvious once I got there.

But she didn't respond anyway, and when I looked at the screen I saw she'd already hung up.

· · · · · ● · ● · · ·

Sewell Park was barely a mile away from the hotel, giving me a chance to get in a much-needed walk to somewhat clear my head. But the morning heat had already kicked in, and I'd started to wish I'd called a cab once I was halfway there. And by the time I arrived at the park, sweat had soaked through my shirt.

The kids screaming at the playground was too much for my tired ears so early in the morning. It looked like a lot of them, fifteen, twenty kids, screaming while the handful of caretakers standing around didn't seem to be paying any of the screeching monsters much attention. Every adult seemed to have their heads in their phones, somehow able to block out the noise.

I continued past the playground, the sounds from the kids fading into the background. I crossed a small parking lot and went past a small sign for the Miami River where I stopped, trying to appear casual, waiting for Kathy. There were a few people out, walking along a paved path along the river, but none of them turned out to be Kathy. I looked at my watch, and it had already been forty minutes since her call.

I looked on the other side of the river, then toward the parking lot and out toward a road where more cars were parked.

An older couple sat on the edge of the river in folding lawn chairs, drinking from silver travel mugs but not saying much if anything at all to each other. They were both looking at their phones.

It wasn't exactly quiet, with boats moving slowly on the freshwater river, and faint sounds from cars traveling on what I believed was the Seventeenth-Street Bridge.

I checked my phone, to see if Kathy had called.

She hadn't.

A full-sized SUV pulled into one of the parking lot and backed into a space. I assumed Kathy would be driving her white Mercedes, but it was nowhere in sight.

I walked farther down the river, toward what looked like an old foundation. A sign explained that it'd been what remained of the guest house, owned by General Samuel Crocker Lawrence. According to the sign, the general had purchased the property in 1887. The park was named after Miami Mayor E.G. Sewell.

I gazed out at the river, looking across at the buildings on the other side. I didn't know if there were parking lots over there, but had to assume she'd let me know where she was, and would at least call me once she arrived.

I looked back toward the SUV in the parking lot. A man stepped out of the driver's side and started in my direction.

The man wore a baseball cap and sunglasses, and I couldn't help but be suspicious.

I started to walk away, in the opposite direction with the river to my right, trying not to look back until I stopped, glanced over my shoulder and saw the man continuing toward me with long, purposeful steps.

I picked up my pace and looked back.

I was pretty sure this guy was coming after me. And instead of running away, I stopped and waited.

"Can I help you?" I said.

The man lifted his shirt and pulled a gun from his waistband, pointing it toward me. "Where is it?" he said.

"Excuse me? Where is *what*?"

The man pulled the visor on his hat down tight over his sunglasses. "Don't play games," he said.

"I don't know what you're talking about," I said.

He pointed his gun at my face.

"Whoa," I said, raising both hands in front of my shoulders. "Let's just talk about this. I'm not armed, so..."

The man stepped closer, the gun still raised.

But before he said another word, I charged toward him, driving my shoulder into his chest. But as soon as I made contact he wrapped his arms around me. We both stumbled and crashed into the river, wrestling in waist-deep water.

I got one arm free and threw a punch, hitting him so hard in his steel-like jaw I thought I'd broken my hand. But he barely budged, other than trying to catch his sunglasses floating down the river.

He pulled his soaked baseball hat down low over his head with one hand, as if trying to hide his identity, then took a swing at me with the other. He had a gun in his hand, and when he hit me in the ear it sounded like something inside my head had exploded.

I reached for his gun, trying to get it free from his grasp, and a shot fired into the air.

There were screams from all over the park.

He grabbed a clump of my hair and had a fistful of it, yanking and twisting so hard it burned. I had no choice but to let go of the gun, grabbing his thick wrists with both hands, trying to get free.

But he fired his gun again, this time into the water.

I felt an immediate, sharp pain in my leg. The water around me turned red.

The man pushed my head into the water, holding my head back, and lifted his gun, about to fire.

But I grabbed his shirt and came up hard, driving my elbow where no man wants to be hit. He let out a scream, then stumbled back in the water. As he fell backward, he raised his gun again like he was about to fire.

He was out of my reach, and I thought for sure it was the end. I closed my eyes and ducked into the water.

A shot rang out, but I felt nothing.

I came up and watched the man collapse into the water, then float face down past me.

I looked myself over. Other than the pain in my leg, I was pretty sure I hadn't been shot a second time. I glanced around the park, but saw nobody. Not a single soul anywhere.

The man had already floated far enough away from me there was no point trying to help him, although it had crossed my mind.

I walked out of the water, and out of the corner of my eye saw movement from behind a tree not far from where I stood. "Who's there?" I said, wiping the water from my face.

Kathy stepped out into the open. She had a gun down by her side. "Let's go!" she said, her voice loud enough so I could hear, but hushed. I was still unsure what had just happened, but followed after her.

She had started to run, but when I did the same, the pain in my leg intensified.

"Wait up!" I yelled, but she didn't seem to listen.

I pushed myself to continue, slowing only once I saw her white Mercedes parked in a space along what I believed was South River Drive.

Kathy had already gotten into the car and was behind the wheel, engine running. She was visibly shaken.

I slid onto the passenger seat and closed the door.

"What the hell just happened?" I said.

She took off from the parking space without a word, cutting into the heavy morning traffic without a second thought. Horns blew and tires squealed, Kathy gripping the wheel so tight her knuckles were white.

"Are you going to tell me what just came off back there?" I said.

Kathy had the pedal floored, weaving in and out of cars in front of us. "I don't know," is all she said, glancing at my bloodied leg. "What happened?"

"I think he shot me," I said, as if I didn't know for sure.

The blood was dripping to my shoe and onto the floor mat under it. "I need a towel," I said.

"What about a doctor?" she said, her eyes on the road now. The tires squealed, Kathy cutting the wheel with a sharp turn onto Northwest Fourteenth.

The pain was sharp but not horrible. It burned more than anything at that point and didn't exactly feel like I'd been shot. Sadly, I knew too well what that felt like.

"Do you have anything in here?" I said, looking at the back seat. "I'm ruining your floor."

She looked like she didn't know what to say, her eyes shifting between me and the road ahead. "You need a doctor," she said, then looked me in the eye. "Your face. It's so white." She slammed her foot down on the gas, as if she wasn't going fast enough already.

"We don't need to get pulled over," I said.

"I'm taking you to the hospital."

"No, it's fine," I said. "I just need something to wrap it up."

"A Band-Aid?" she said.

"Maybe a little more than that," I said.

Chapter 17

Kathy came out of Fred's Pharmacy with two white paper bags and a bath towel rolled up under her arm. She opened the passenger door and crouched down next to me outside the car, in the parking lot. "Let me look," she said, one hand on my knee, the other reaching for my bloody leg.

I thought about what had happened at the park while she was inside, and couldn't really get any of it to add up.

She pulled a pair of scissors from the bag.

"Are you sure you've never seen that man before?" I said.

She glanced up at me and proceeded to cut my pants. "I told you I hadn't. How would I know who he is."

"But you showed up to meet me... and had a gun?"

She almost acted as if she hadn't heard me, continuing with the scissors, cutting my pant leg all the way up to my knee. The bleeding had somewhat stopped. She finally glanced up at me. "My brother was killed. And someone's already come after us. You think I'm going to walk around like there's nothing to worry about?"

She reached for the towel she'd bought, pressing it against the wound on my leg, then took my hand to hold it in place. "Keep the pressure on," she said, then pulled out a roll of bandages and the medical tape. "Let's get your leg outside the car," she said, again looking over her shoulder into the lot.

"All right," I said. "Then how did this guy know I was at that park?" I looked around the lot, afraid someone would walk by or see us and end up asking questions I didn't want to answer.

She said, "Maybe he followed you?"

I thought about it, but would have of course noticed someone following me, especially considering the fact I'd walked from the hotel.

She lifted the towel from my leg and got a good look at my wound. "It's a pretty good one," she said. "But it doesn't look as bad as I thought. Are you sure you were shot?"

"No, I'm not," I said. "But it would have to be a real coincidence, this guy shoots into the water and I cut it on something else at the exact moment."

She grabbed the jug from behind her, pouring water over the wound. I didn't question what she was doing, because she looked like she had a pretty good handle on it.

Kathy continued her work to clean me up, then wrapped the bandage around my leg several times, then went over it with tape.

"Thank you," I said, standing up from the car. "It feels good."

She picked up the bandage wrappers from the ground and threw it all in one of the bags, taking it all over to the trash can in front of the pharmacy's entrance.

Coming back to the car, she used the same jug of water to clean her hands, then poured water into another towel and used it to clean some of the blood inside the car.

"What I don't understand," I said, "is what this guy wanted from me." I looked at Kathy, walking around to the driver's side. "You think it has something to do with Brock? Maybe he told someone he gave me something?"

Kathy went around and got in on the driver's side. "Get in."

"Where are we going?"

She stared out at me from behind the wheel. "Just get in."

I slid into the passenger seat, being careful with my leg. I said, "Did you see what I did with my phone?"

Kathy adjusted the rearview mirror without a reply.

I looked on the floor and on either side of my seat, and saw it to my left, by the seat belt latch, shoved between the seat and the center console. I reached in and pulled it out, tapping what first appeared to be a blank screen. "You've got to be kidding me," I said. I held the power button, hoping it would come back to life.

But I was out of luck.

"My phone's dead," I said. "From the water."

She shifted the car into drive, but before we left the parking lot, kept her foot on the brake and turned to me. "Do you trust me?" She looked back at me from the driver's seat.

"Trust you?" I hesitated to answer. "I appreciate what you did for me here. You probably saved my life, then cleaned me up pretty good."

She held her gaze, waiting for my reply.

"I'm sorry. But I'm not sure I do."

· · · · · • · · · ·

We drove past the airport and Kathy turned onto Northwest Twenty-Fifth, driving into the parking lot of a place with a worn sign that said Save-More Storage. Under it, read Safe and Secure.

I wondered if "save more" meant you'd save money storing your things there, or if they were trying to encourage people to keep their junk, and save more stuff so they could pay to store it.

I was never one to own a lot of things. I didn't want the trouble, and living on a boat didn't give me much choice. It never crossed my mind to own something I'd have to keep in storage.

The place didn't look new at all, half the bricks on the building cracked or missing. It was enclosed by a tall chain-link fence with barbed wire on top of it. It reminded me of a time I had to jump a fence to another storage place in Jacksonville, that looked eerily similar. I'd even, at the time, torn my leg trying to climb over it. It gave me a feeling of déjà vu.

The only thing Kathy told me on the ride over was that Brock had given her a sealed package the morning before he was killed, but told her nothing about it. He needed her to hold on to it for him.

She *claimed* to know nothing about the contents, and how Brock refused to give her any details. She said, "I didn't open it until after I found out he was dead."

There were no other cars at the storage place.

Kathy turned into an empty parking space by a small building I guess was an office. But it was dark inside, with the lights off. She reached under her seat and popped the trunk open, stepping outside the car.

I got out and watched her reach into the trunk, then close the lid.

She had a large white envelope in her hand, the top of it torn open.

"What's inside?" I said.

She reached into the envelope and came out with a piece of paper, handing it to me.

It had the numbers 8-3-0-2 written on it, in black ink.

I looked at the chain-link entrance gate, where a keypad was attached to the post keeping it closed. "You want me to try it?"

She nodded, and we both cautiously walked to the gate, where I leaned in close so I could see the dirty, worn-out numbers on the keypad.

I tapped 8-3-0-2 and heard a click, then pulled open the gate. "After you," I said, handing her the piece of paper.

"You sure you have no idea what's in here?" I said.

She shook her head. "I know you don't believe anything I say, but it's the truth. He didn't tell me anything."

I walked in after her and pulled the gate closed. "What else is in there?"

She reached into the envelope and removed two separate keys, each attached to a key ring with a plastic tag that had numbers written on it.

Kathy handed me the first one, with the number 1017 on it, this time written in blue marker. The units outside all had garage doors with the unit number attached to the brick exterior wall, to the right of each door.

We continued until we got to the end of the building, turned the corner and found unit 1017.

There was a Master lock I opened with the key, lifting the door.

Kathy stood next to me and we both looked at five washing machines, three clothes dryers, a couple of microwaves, and at least a dozen large boxes with televisions inside.

We were both quiet at first.

I said, "Did this all belong to Brock?"

Kathy just looked at me, but didn't answer.

"Is it all stolen?" I gave her a quick look.

Kathy shrugged. "I told you, I know nothing about it."

"But you must realize there's a chance this is what got him killed, right?" I glanced over my shoulder when I thought I heard something out toward the front of the building. "Wait here," I said, walking to the corner. Leaning against the bricks, I saw someone from a parked car walk into the office.

"Someone's here," I said.

Kathy looked worried. "What should we do?"

I pulled the garage door closed and locked it, handing Kathy back the key. "I think we should get out of here."

"Wait," she said, reaching into the envelope. She pulled out another key with the same plastic tag on the key ring.

It had the number 2132 written on it.

I looked up the side of the building, at the second-story windows. "I guess we could go see what else is here," I said, taking another look at the key with the numbers on the tag. "There must be more units upstairs."

She looked back and forth, then walked toward the back of the building.

I looked around for cameras, but didn't see any.

"This way," Kathy said, heading round the back.

I followed her until we got to a heavy steel door. There was a keypad to the right of it, on the brick wall, and I tried the same code we used to get in through the gate at the entrance.

Sure enough, it worked.

Inside, there was a strong, musty odor, with the air much more damp and humid than it was outside.

We continued up the stairs to the second story and stopped at a plate-glass door that wasn't locked.

On the other side of it was a long hallway. We went through the door and down the hall, our shoes slapping the floor with each step, the only other sound coming from the slow, whirring sound of large industrial fans high up on the exposed ceiling above.

Kathy got ahead of me and continued until she stopped halfway down the hall at one of the storage units on the left. She slid a key in the lock and lifted the door.

Unit number 2123.

Inside was an old oak desk pushed up against the back wall. There was a dirty, cracked leather desk chair on wheels pushed in the opposite corner from the desk.

"What is this?" I said. "Someone's office?"

We both stood looking into the small unit, and Kathy reached inside the envelope she had in her hand. "There's another key," she said, then moved toward the desk, crouching down with the key she had in her hand. She unlocked the file drawer on the right.

I was still outside the unit, and turned to look down the hall when I heard what sounded like a door had opened and closed. But I didn't see anyone. When I looked back inside the unit,

Kathy had a small .38 revolver with a wooden handle in her hand.

"Is that yours?" I said.

She glanced back at me over her shoulder, shaking her head. "It was in the drawer." She reached back inside the drawer and took out what looked like a brick wrapped in white paper and sealed with clear tape. She put it on top of the desk, reached inside and removed another package, the same size and sealed the same way.

She took nine more packages from that drawer and placed them on the desk, turning to me with one in her hand, then tossing it to me. "Can you open it?"

I looked it over. I wondered, at first, if it was drugs. Cocaine, maybe. Or heroine.

I picked at the end of the tape wrapped around the package, until finally getting the end free, unraveling the package. I unfolded what turned out to be a large white envelope similar to the one that held the keys to the storage units.

"What is it?" Kathy said, but asked in a way I wasn't exactly convinced she didn't know. We still hadn't discussed anything about her lying to the cops, or me telling them the truth. It was as if we both wanted to pretend that's not what happened.

Kathy held the gun in her hand and I said, "Probably best you put that down."

I opened the clasp on the envelope's flap and stopped, before looking inside. I reached in and came out with a stack of what turned out to be hundred dollar bills.

A lot of them.

The bills were banded together and sealed with a white paper strip. "Do you expect me to believe you didn't know this was all in here?" I said.

She shook her head. "Why would I lie?"

"You mean, the way you lied to the cops?" I said.

She stood, staring back at me. "Do you really want to get into that?" she said. "Brock trusted you, and you told them—"

"I told them what I thought they needed to know, to protect him. To protect you both. Clearly, I was a little late."

Kathy rolled her eyes and looked over the bundle of money in her hand, then pulled seven more bundles out of the desk drawer. She kept her back to me.

"That's got to be close to a hundred grand," I said. "Maybe more."

Without saying a word to me, she pulled the large drawer out and placed it on top of the desk, putting the package back inside it.

"What are you doing?" I said.

Kathy lifted the drawer and stepped past me, out of the storage unit.

"Kathy?" I said, grabbing her by the arm. "What are you doing?"

She yanked her arm from me. "What's it look like I'm doing?"

"We're not taking this money," I said.

She started walking away. "Well, I'm not leaving it here. Brock obviously gave me these keys for a reason. This is... This money belonged to him."

"You don't know that?" I said. "And if it did, it surely wasn't his to begin with. It's stolen." I followed after her.

"We can split it," she said. "Me and you."

I stepped around in front of her and grabbed the drawer full of money. I could see the greed in her eyes. The old Kathy was back. Or maybe she'd never left.

"If we're doing anything, we're going to go to the cops." I carried the drawer back to the unit and slid it into the desk.

"What's wrong with you?" she said. "Nobody has to know anything."

"We're probably being watched right now," I said, without any real reason to believe that. But I had a feeling…

"What do you even need this for? You married Luke, and you made it perfectly clear he's got plenty of money. I assume that's why you married him, isn't it?"

Her eyes narrowed, as if she didn't like what I'd said. "I love Luke."

"I didn't say you didn't. But…" I took her arm and helped her out of the unit. "Trust me, Kathy. This is the right thing to do," I said, reaching up for the door. "At least until we figure out who this belongs to." Before I closed the door, I noticed the gun left out on the desk. I stepped back in and put it back into the drawer, then stepped out and closed the door.

Kathy wouldn't even look at me, walking ahead in a huff, heading for the door to the stairs.

I locked the unit and hurried after her. "Don't you want to know who killed Brock?" I said. "This could help the cops find the answer."

Kathy went through the door and continued down the stairs ahead of me, but stopped once we got outside. "You think it matters to them? You think they really care who killed Brock?"

"The police?" I said. "Why wouldn't they?"

Kathy paused, then turned away, continuing toward the exit.

I continued after her. "Kathy, wait." I looked toward Northwest Twenty-Fifth, along the front of the building, and saw a vehicle that appeared to be stopped. But then it drove away, taking off before I could get a good enough look at it.

"Did you see what kind of car that was?" I said.

Kathy shook her head, acting like a child who didn't get what she wanted. We walked outside of the fence and she continued to her car. "Let's go," she said. "I'll drop you off at the hotel."

Chapter 18

Kathy hadn't said a word to me on the ride back, turning off Northwest Thirteenth and into the hotel parking lot. She continued around the side of the building and toward the back.

"What are you doing?" I said.

"I can't have anyone see me dropping you off," she said.

"Like who?" I said, glancing at the sign that read SERVICE ENTRANCE where she'd stopped and put the Mercedes in park.

She said, "I think it's just better we're not seen together." She wouldn't look me in the eye, or say specifically who she was worried about. Her eyes were straight ahead, until she finally turned to me. "In fact, I think at this point, maybe it's best we stay clear of each other for a little while."

"Because I wouldn't let you take that money?" I said. I wanted to laugh, but the mood obviously didn't call for it. "I came down here to help you and your brother. You asked me to. Or did you forget?"

"Well, he's gone now," she said. "I need to think about what I'm going to do from here."

I was a little confused about what she was saying. "What about what happened at the park this morning? We don't even know what the cops know about it at this point. And, in case you forgot, you shot that man. What if he's dead?"

"I shot him to save your life," she said, as if the implications didn't matter.

"Right. I know that," I said. "But the cops don't. Who knows what witnesses saw or what anyone told them. There could be video of—"

"What am I supposed to do?" she said, coming off as someone who was more annoyed than worried.

"And what am *I* supposed to do? You expect me to lie?"

"You can't tell them about the money," she said.

I thought about it, staring back, watching her with her eyes closed, hands on the shifter like she was ready to go. "I think you need to come clean. You need to tell them the truth about everything." I pushed open the passenger door. "But you can't expect me to lie for you," I said, stepping out onto the asphalt, leaning in to look in at Kathy. "I'm sorry. I can't put myself in a position like that."

The look on her face was clear: She didn't like what I'd said. "I need to go," she said, shifting the car into drive. "Luke's going to be wondering where I am. He gets suspicious when I don't tell him where I've gone."

"Suspicious?"

She shrugged. "Jealous, more than anything."

"I hope he knows he has nothing to worry about," I said.

She held her gaze, a slight smile on her face. "He gets jealous of handsome men."

"Well, then, I guess he has nothing to worry about."

She turned from me, looking out the driver-side window. "He knows about us."

"Us?" I said, and huffed out a laugh. "Kathy, there is no 'us.' There hasn't been an 'us' in twelve years. What did you tell him?"

"The real reason he doesn't trust me is, well..." She cleared her throat. "I had an affair."

I straightened up outside the car, looking toward the sky. I wasn't surprised. "That pretty much explains why he can't trust you."

"It was nothing, really. But we almost got divorced over it. And Luke... I thought he was going to kill the guy. He actually went to his house, dragged him out to the front lawn in front of his wife, and—"

"I don't need to hear any of this," I said. "It's really none of my business." I looked at my dead phone. "If you need to reach me, I think you'll have to call the front desk."

I started to close the door when Kathy said my name.

I ducked my head down to look inside. "Yeah?"

"You're not going to call the cops, are you?"

I hesitated a moment. I hadn't quite made up my mind, or really thought about what I was supposed to do. "I think maybe we should both go down there." I looked at my watch, which luckily—unlike my phone—was still working. "I have to go down to Miami-Dade headquarters, find out what's up with my friend's car."

"Your friend's car?"

"The BMW. It's Billy's."

She nodded. "Oh, right."

"Maybe we can kill two birds with one stone, if you want to take a ride down with me?"

"You mean you need a ride?" she said. "Let me get home and see if Luke's around first." She looked at her cell phone. "I'm actually surprised he hasn't called me."

I glanced at the floor on the passenger side. We'd managed to clean it up pretty good, although Kathy had decided to throw the bloody floor mat in a dumpster. "Sorry about the mess," I said, and closed the door.

·····•·•····

I stepped off the elevator and poked my head out before stepping off. My shoes were still wet, each step making a sloshy squeak on the carpeted floor.

I turned the corner and saw two cops down the hall, standing in front of a door. At first, I wasn't sure if they were outside my room, but once I got a few steps closer, I realized they were.

"Can I help you?" I said, approaching the two officers.

They both turned, looked me over, then fixed their gaze on my cut pants and the bloody bandage around my leg.

"It's nothing," I said with a grin.

The taller of the two Miami-Dade officers said, "Are you Henry Walsh?"

"I guess that depends," I said, although I knew I wasn't likely in any kind of place to be playing games. I reconsidered my answer. "Yes, I'm Henry. Can I help you with something?"

The tall one said, "We need to ask you some questions."

"Questions?" I said. "I like questions."

The two cops looked at each other and the tall one said, "Would you mind coming with us? Downtown?"

"What's downtown?" I said, even though I knew what he meant. I couldn't help myself.

"We'd like you to come to the station," the tall one said. "One of our detectives is waiting for you."

I thought about it. "Detective Collins?" I said. "She couldn't come here herself?"

The short one of the two shook his head. "Detective Helms."

"I don't know a detective by that name," I said. "What's it about?"

The two paused, as if they weren't sure they should answer.

The tall one said, "You were spotted at Save-More Storage a little while ago."

I tried to hold my swallow, looking from one cop to the other. "So?"

The cop sighed, "You asked me what it's about. And I'm telling you. Detective Helms will explain the situation."

"So you're asking me to go with you, because I was at a storage place?"

"Mr. Walsh, we are only asking. But we hope you'll cooperate."

I looked at my watch and couldn't understand how these two showed up at the hotel so fast, when Kathy and I had only left the storage place within the hour.

I said, "How'd you find me?" I said. "How'd you know I was there?"

The taller office said, "The building has been under surveillance."

The shorter one hadn't said much of anything, stepping away from us for a moment to use the two-way radio clipped to his vest. He walked far enough away I couldn't hear what he was saying.

"Just so I'm clear," I said. "I'm not under arrest?"

"No sir," the tall one said. "Detective Helms is waiting."

I looked at the door to my room. "You mind if I go in and change out of these pants?"

The shorter one turned back to us, stepped over and looked down at my leg and the blood-covered shoe. "You want to tell us what happened?"

"I really don't," I said. "It's nothing. I snagged it on something."

The two gave each other a quick glance, then the tall one nodded. "Hurry up."

I pulled my card key and slid it through the remote lock, but of course it wouldn't open. I tried twice, shaking the handle. I glanced back at the two cops watching me. "I don't know why we can't just use regular keys." I tried it again, sliding the card through the lock, and this time it opened. I slipped inside and looked back at the two cops still watching me. "Be right out." I closed the door, reached into my pocket and checked my phone. It still didn't work, and at that point I knew it was likely dead for good.

I thought about calling Alex, but thought I'd wait to see what was ahead for me, down at the station. I thought about the fact they had the place under surveillance, and wondered if they'd grabbed Kathy out in the parking lot. I wouldn't know either way, since I didn't have a phone. I didn't even know her number offhand. The dead phone in my hand was useless.

I opened my duffel bag and pulled out a pair of pants. I would've preferred shorts, but didn't need to show off my bandaged leg and introduce any more questions than I apparently already had coming.

I slipped into the bathroom and threw cold water on my face, running my wet hands through my hair. Looking in the mirror, I looked like I'd aged a few years since I first arrived in Miami. The bags under my eyes... the touch of gray showing up in my unshaved face.

I wiped my hands and headed back out into the hall, where both cops were in conversation, but stopped as soon as I stepped out of the room.

"I was just thinking," I said. "What if I refuse to go?"

The taller, older-looking one said, "I don't think that's a good idea. We can always come back, but you won't have a choice at that point."

"Can you at least be a little more specific about what this is all about?" I said.

"We already told you, sir," said the shorter cop. He was stocky, with a thick neck like he spent his off days in the gym.

I paused, thinking through my limited options, then finally nodded. It wasn't worth stirring the pot. "Okay."

The three of us walked down the hall and turned the corner to the elevator.

I said, "What'd you say is the detective's name? Helms?"

The shorter cop nodded.

I wondered what would've happened to Detective Collins. I had to guess she was the one who'd told them where to find me, but I also didn't understand why she wouldn't just come get me herself. Or why this Helms guy was now involved.

Maybe it was an entirely different case, or simply related but not specific to the homicide. I could only guess.

Chapter 19

I WAS ESCORTED UP the steps of the Miami-Dade police station, through the glass doors at the main entrance and through another door that led us to a small but open area with what looked like at least a dozen cops. Half of them were at desks, the others standing, some sipping from Styrofoam cups hanging around like they had nothing to do.

One of the officers I drove with had disappeared as soon as we got there, the other—the shorter one with all the muscle—walked ahead of me through the room and down a hall. He stopped at an open door and gestured for me to walk in ahead of him.

"Take a seat," he said, nodding toward a long steel table bolted to the floor in the middle of the windowless room. "Detective Helms will be with you in a moment." He turned for the door, then looked back at me. "You want a coffee?"

I thought about it, then nodded. "Yeah, sure."

The officer's last name, I'd learned, was Lapinski. Another Polish cop out of the dozens I'd met over the years. I don't know what it was, but it seemed like a lot of cops were of Polish descent. Maybe it did just seem that way.

He closed the door behind him when he left the room and, I felt, for a moment, like the questioning wasn't going to be as voluntary as they made it sound.

A video camera on the wall had a red light on it and was pointed toward the table. A round clock hung on one wall, but nothing else.

The fake leather cushion on the seat was worn and flattened, with a hole in the side of it where it looked like someone had picked away at it and tore out pieces of foam.

The phone in the middle of the table had three tiny lights flashing, each with a different set of numbers next to it.

The door opened, and Officer Lapinski walked in with a foam cup in each hand, sipping from one as he placed the other in front of me. "Cream?" he said.

I picked up the hot cup, shaking my head. "This is good. Thank you."

He gave a nod and again turned for the door. "Helms'll be in, in a few minutes." He looked back one more time before closing the door.

I sat, alone now, and gave a nod and a smile to the camera. I wondered if there was a chance this detective, Detective Helms, was talking to someone else. Maybe they'd already talked to Kathy, knowing right then there was a serious risk we'd both end up giving different stories.

I sipped the coffee, but could smell the burntness as soon as I had it up near my nose. It was too hot to get a good taste of it, but it was more likely than not it wasn't very good either way. I don't know what it was about cops. They never had good coffee at the station. Maybe that's why they spent so much time in coffee shops.

The door opened and a middle-aged, balding man with a disheveled look had his eyes on a folder he held with both hands.

He dropped the folder on the table and sat across from me, looking at the contents before finally raising his gaze. "So, you're Henry Walsh, huh?" He gave a quick nod. "Gary Helms," he said, as if trying to make it like we were on the same level. "Thanks for coming in."

"I'm not sure I had a choice," I said.

The detective grinned and inched his chair closer to the table, once again scanning over the documents in the folder. "So..." He paused, eyes still on whatever he had in that folder. "You know why you're here?"

"To answer your questions," I said.

"You were spotted coming out of a storage facility we've had our eyes on for a few weeks."

"Was I the only one coming out of the place?" I said.

He shook his head. "You're the only one who's friends with Brock Mason."

"Oh," I said.

"And you happened to be there with his sister, so..."

I didn't respond.

Helms said, "I understand you had some kind of relationship with her?"

"A relationship?" I shrugged.

Helms was clearly a bit grizzled, appearing like he'd been around the block a few times, and back again. I had a feeling he wasn't easily fooled, and playing games with him was a short-term solution.

"What's the crime?" I said.

He gave me a look, like he wasn't sure he had an answer.

I said, "I mean... Do you think I've done something wrong here? Or..."

"I haven't said that," the detective said.

After a long pause, he slid his chair back, the leg tips scraping on the hard vinyl floor. "We've had our eye on that storage facility for the past few weeks. It's not uncommon these storage businesses are used for criminal activity. Storing stolen goods. Money. Drugs. When we got a tip a couple of weeks back, we thought we'd keep an eye on the place, see if anything came up. Nobody's been in or out of there at all. Not until today."

I waited for more, but decided I'd just keep quiet.

Helms grinned. "So, you want to tell me what you and your old girlfriend were doing there? From what we were able to tell, you went in empty-handed. But whether or not either of you came out with something is another story."

I shook my head. "We took nothing from there."

"Am I supposed to believe you?" Helms said.

I leaned on the table and looked the man in the eye. "I can't tell you what you should or shouldn't believe. But that's the truth."

He got up from the table, straightening his tie.

I said, "What I don't understand is how you had those two cops over to the hotel so fast. I'd only been gone from the storage place, I don't know, maybe a half hour, at most."

"You say it like we don't know who you are," he said.

I decided, before I'd continue, maybe it would be best to keep my mouth shut. Clearly they were suspicious of me. One thing I hadn't heard anything about was what had happened in the park. I assumed how it had all gone down, in broad daylight, would at least be newsworthy. I still didn't know if the man Kathy had shot was dead or alive.

But I wasn't about to ask.

"Okay," he said, taking a pen and spiral-bound notepad from his shirt pocket. He flipped the cover over. "Let's get down to the million-dollar question."

"I was wondering why you hadn't asked," I said.

"Then, why don't you tell me," the detective said. "What was it you were doing at Save-More Storage today?"

I thought for a moment before responding. I was still on the fence about coming clean versus feeding him a lie. And without knowing what the detective already knew, I had to be careful about my answer. The last thing I needed to do was implicate myself for something I had nothing to do with, and knew little about.

I said, "Why wouldn't you just get a search warrant, go in there and look for yourself?"

"It doesn't work like that," he said. "Not yet."

"You can't just get a search warrant, go through the place?"

"Mr. Walsh. If you could please just tell me what it was you were doing there, you would save us a lot of trouble. And as far as we know, Kathy Arnold does not have a unit in that building. At least not one registered under her own name. Neither did Brock Mason."

"Her husband?" I said.

The detective shook his head. "No."

I wasn't sure what I was supposed to say to this man. Of course, the easy thing to do—and maybe the right thing to do— would be to tell him what Kathy showed me. But I'm not sure he'd believe me if I told him I knew nothing about who any of it belonged to.

I never promised Kathy I'd keep quiet, although that was before the cops showed up, waiting for me outside my room at the hotel.

I said, "Does any of this have something to do with the recent murders?"

"You mean, your buddy? And his so-called girlfriend?"

"And Steve Rogers," I said. "Jillian's ex-husband?"

The detective shrugged. "Honestly, we hadn't made any kind of connection until today, when we saw you and your girlfriend coming out of that storage facility."

"She's not my girlfriend," I said, knowing the detective was trying to get under my skin.

"Well, you knew who I was talking about," he said, a big grin on his face. "So, clearly..."

"Clearly nothing," I said. "There's nothing between us. And I'd appreciate it if you—"

"Relax, Mr. Walsh," the detective said, turning to look toward the door when it opened.

Officer Lapinski poked his head into the room. "Gary, can I have a word with you?"

Detective Helms nodded, but didn't move from his chair.

Lapinski didn't look like he knew if he should talk, or if Helms was going to follow him out into the hall. Lapinski went ahead with what he had to say. "They've located Kathy Arnold's vehicle; I don't have the exact location yet. But it appears there may've been foul play. The driver-side door was left wide open. No sign of Mrs. Arnold."

"No sign?" Helms said. "What's that supposed to mean? Where the hell is she?"

Lapinski shrugged and shook his head. "It's in a neighborhood, dead-end street, in North Miami. I don't have all the details yet, but there's blood in the vehicle."

I didn't mention there was a chance the blood could have been mine. If I did, I'd open up a whole other can of worms.

"What are you saying?" I said. "Is she missing? Or..."

"You know what happened to her?" Helms said, eyes on me now.

"I already told you I don't," I said. "I saw her at the hotel, as I said, when she dropped me off."

"Did she say where she was going?" Helms said.

I had to think for a moment. "I thought she said she was on her way home."

Chapter 20

I drove with Detective Helms in his Dodge Durango heading to North Miami, turning onto Northeast Sixteenth Avenue and passing a sign at the entrance to a park, reading Enchanted Elaine Gordon Park. The next turn brought us to Enchanted Forest Place, a residential street with an abundance of overgrown vegetation on either side of the road. Single-family houses were spread out with spacious yards filled with numerous tall oak trees covered in Spanish moss.

The detective stopped behind Kathy's white Mercedes, the trunk open and parked along the heavily wooded area between two houses. Three Miami-Dade police vehicles were on the scene, officers standing outside the car.

I had the door open, jumping out before he fully stopped.

The driver-side door to the Mercedes was also open, one officer inside, going through the car. He turned and looked back at me as I approached and stood behind him.

"What have you found?" I said.

He stepped back from the car and gave me a confused look. "Who the hell are you?"

"Henry Walsh," I said, as if that would clear anything up.

The officer turned when Detective Helms came up behind me, said, "Who is this guy?"

"Nobody," he said, slipping past me to get a look inside the car. "Find anything?"

I looked toward the other officers, walking along the wooded area with another man in plain clothes who'd glanced my way when I said my name. At first, I thought he was a cop. But I quickly realized who it was.

Kathy's husband looked older than in the photos of him I'd found online, thinner now with gray hair coming out from under his stained baseball cap. He wore work boots and faded jeans and an untucked plaid shirt, sleeves rolled up past his elbows.

I assumed the tank-sized pickup truck was his.

Luke Arnold narrowed his eyes, staring back at me. He held a wad of something in behind his lower lip, then shot a thick stream of brown spit from his mouth to the ground and started toward me.

I remembered how Kathy had mentioned her husband reminded her of me, and I tried to make sense of her statement.

Luke shoved one of the officers out of his way and started toward me with long steps, fists clenched. Without a word, he threw a right hook I wasn't expecting, and followed it with a punch to my head that felt like someone had tossed a brick at me from five feet away.

I stumbled back and fell to one knee, getting right back to my feet before he came at me again with a wild swing. But this time I ducked and came up with a punch, hitting him in a place few men deserve to be struck.

Luke let out a yelp, like an injured dog, and collapsed just as the officers had grabbed me, trying to get us apart.

I wiped blood from my mouth with the back of my hand, my right ear burning and ringing from the punch he landed that felt like a mule had kicked me. "Nice to finally meet," I said, watching the cops help Luke to his feet, holding him back.

Detective Helms was one of the cops holding me, his fingers digging into the crux of my arm. "Christ," he said with somewhat of a growl. "What's the matter with you two?"

"You two?" I said. "Didn't you see what just happened?"

Luke Arnold's chest was moving in and out with his heavy, labored breathing. He had a look on his face like he wasn't quite done with me.

"What'd you do to her?" he yelled, teeth clenched, the wad of soaked, spit-filled tobacco on the ground between us.

Helms finally eased up his grip and stood between us with one of the Miami-Dade officers next to him. "What makes you think he had something to do with this?" Helms said, face-to-face with Luke now.

"He's been after her since he came down here," Luke said, his eyes still on me. "You son of a bitch... What'd you do to her?"

Helms said, "I don't believe he's done anything to your wife. He was with me."

"You know that for a fact?" Luke said.

Detective Helms seemed to hesitate, glancing back at me. He didn't exactly answer. "Mr. Arnold, please. I'm going to need you to get ahold of yourself."

One of the other officers stepped around Luke. "We've talked to a couple of the neighbors nearby. Nobody heard, or saw, a thing."

A maroon vehicle pulled up and parked behind Helms. Detective Mia Collins stepped out, with her phone to her ear. She stood outside her door, nodding into the phone, then finally hung up and continued toward us.

"What've we got?" she said, glancing into the car before turning to me. "Do you know anything about this?"

I shook my head. "No."

"I understand you were with her earlier today, were you not?"

"You were with her?" Luke Arnold yelled. "See? I told you, this son of a bitch—"

"Get him out of here!" Detective Helms said, pointing at Luke Arnold.

The officer led him away, over toward the big truck.

I said, "I was at the station with—"

"I know where you were," Collins said. "But I mean *before* you were spotted at the Save-More Storage. Were you not with her earlier today?"

I said, "no," then glanced at Kathy's husband standing with two cops by his truck, a permanent snarl on his face, watching me. I had to guess he didn't know much of anything about what had occurred earlier in the day with me and Kathy. But something had led him to believe I was somehow responsible for her disappearance.

Collins walked around the other side of the car and slipped on a pair of rubber gloves she had tucked in her blue jacket. She opened the passenger-side door, where I knew right away that she'd see my blood from earlier. "Did we get a sample of this?"

Detective Helms walked around to the other side of the Mercedes and said something to her, almost in a whisper, and the two looked across the top of the car, right at me.

Collins walked around to where I stood, her gaze down. "What happened to your leg?"

"Nothing. Why?"

The detective reached down and lifted my pants from the bottom, enough to where my bandage was exposed.

"Nothing?" she said, looking me in the eye. "Any chance that's your blood over there, inside the car?" She waited, her gaze fixed on mine, arms folded. "You might as well tell the truth, because we'll know if it's yours or not within a few hours."

I swallowed hard, trying to think through my options. But I knew I wasn't in any kind of position to tell her anything but the truth. "Yeah," I said. "It's my blood."

Detective Collins glanced at Helms, as if she'd figured something out, although I didn't see it that way.

A bloodied bandage on my leg meant nothing.

Detective Collins took me by the arm and said to Helms, "I'm going to take a moment with Mr. Walsh," she said, pulling me over to her car where she practically slammed me into the driver-side door. "Listen," she said, her finger in my face. "I understand you've got this thing about working with us—the police. I don't know what it is, or what happened to you somewhere along the line. But this woman is missing. Some of the people here believe you had something to do with it. *All* of us feel you know more than you're letting on."

"I don't know what you want me to tell you," I said. "I had nothing to do with whatever happened to her."

She held her gaze, as if expecting me to crack.

"I don't know where she is," I said. "It's the truth."

Detective Collins said, "You were the last person to be seen with her. Do you know how this looks?"

"I think you just told me," I said. "But I don't know what else to say."

I was close to telling her about what happened in the park, although I was pretty curious why it hadn't somehow become news, considering shots had been fired.

She said, "Can you at least tell me why you haven't told Detective Helms what was inside those storage units?"

I was in a tough spot. There was little reason, at that point, for me to try to hide anything else from her. Protecting Kathy didn't seem to be necessary, now that Kathy was missing. I guess the priorities had shifted from trying to keep her out of trouble to making sure we would find her alive.

"All right," I said. "Kathy didn't tell me anything. I mean, I don't know what she knows, or if she knew what was inside those storage units before we got there or not." I went on to describe what I saw, from the appliances I knew without a doubt were stolen, to the bundles of cash stuffed in the drawer of the desk inside the storage unit.

"Let's go," she said, taking me around to the passenger seat of her car. "I want you to show me exactly what you saw."

Chapter 21

I LOOKED OUT THE passenger window, Detective Collins turning into the parking lot at Save-More Storage. She drove directly to the office, where this time the lights were on with someone clearly inside.

Collins stepped out of the car and looked in at me. "Wait here," She closed the door and headed straight into the office.

I sat for a moment, watching her through the blinds on the other side of the office windows, talking to a man behind the counter.

She'd left the windows open but took the keys. Maybe she was afraid I'd take off in her car. But, either way, it was too hot to sit in there, my skin sticking to the leather seat.

I opened the passenger door and stepped outside and turned when Detective Helms pulled into the parking lot behind the wheel of his Dodge Durango. Looking at him through the windshield, he was on the phone, nodding, listening to whoever was on the other end.

I went over to him but he ignored me at first, then lowered the phone and put down the window. "I'm on a call," he said, rolling his window back up.

Going back over to Detective Collins' car, I leaned against it, looking from Collins inside the office to Helms, who had just gotten out of his Durango. He walked toward me without saying a word, then continued past and went inside the office with Collins.

I straightened up off the car when a white box truck drove around from the back of the building and exited onto the street, speeding past until it was out of sight.

Both detectives appeared to be talking to the man behind the counter, so I decided to walk around the building enclosed by the chain-link fence. Around the side I saw a wide, closed gate. I guessed it was where the truck had just driven out from, but had no way of knowing.

There was an old surveillance camera attached to the side of the brick exterior of the building. But it looked old and somewhat rusty. When I got closer, I could see the lens was shattered. There was glass on the ground below it, but mixed in with dirt and debris, it didn't appear the camera's lens had been recently broken.

"Walsh!" a voice yelled, and I hustled back around to the front of the building.

Collins and Helms and the man from inside the office were all looking toward me when I turned the corner.

"I told you to wait here," Collins said, her hands on her hips.

"Sorry," I said.

She didn't even ask what I was doing.

The man from the office, short and sweaty-looking, not to mention a bit pudgy, had a ring full of keys in his hand.

Collins said to me, "Show us which unit."

All three stared at me.

"I'm not sure I remember the number. But I can show you."

Helms rolled his eyes and shook his head. "You're serious? And you call yourself a detective?"

"I'll know it when I see it," I said. I wasn't sure I liked Helms very much, or his clear lack of respect for me. I wasn't sure either one of the two detectives believed I was being straight with them.

The man from the office led the way, taking us through the locked gate at the front and along the building to the far end. He stopped and looked at me.

"Oh," I said, and stepped ahead of the three. I eyed each unit, trying to remember the number. It wasn't that I'd forgotten, as much as I simply hadn't made a mental note of it. Maybe I should have. Or maybe my memory simply wasn't what it used to be.

But I stopped when we got to unit number 1017. "This one," I said, my eyes on the bottom where the lock had been earlier, when I was there with Kathy.

The problem was, the lock wasn't there now.

The short man from the office gave me a look like I must've been confused. "I don't believe this unit is rented," he said. He bent down and grabbed the door's handle, lifting it until he let go of the door and let it roll up by itself above his head.

I stood, dismayed.

There was nothing inside.

"You've gotta be kidding me," Helms said. "Walsh? I believe you've made a mistake."

"No, this is it," I said. I was sure of it now. "Somebody must've emptied it out."

Helms said, "Didn't you tell us it was loaded with appliances? And televisions?"

"That's *exactly* what was in here," I said.

"And it all just disappeared since this morning?" Detective Collins said. She turned to the man from the office and pointed at the adjacent units. "Can you open these?"

He nodded, holding up a single key. "This is the master."

The man first opened the unit to the left. As he lifted the door we could see it was packed full of what looked like mostly used furniture, including a couch and three or four stained mattresses up against the wall. It had a strong smell, like mothballs.

Helms said, "I assume that's not what you saw earlier?"

I shook my head, nodding back at the empty unit. "I'm telling you, this was it."

The man from the office looked at both Collins and Helms, as if waiting for someone to give the word.

Detective Helms said, "What's in this other one?"

The man crouched down and slid his key in the lock to the door to the right of the empty one. He said, "I believe this one is not rented, either." He raised the door and, sure enough, the unit was empty.

I looked past the parking lot toward the street, a row of trees blocking a clear view. "Did anybody see that box truck leaving here earlier?"

Collins and Helms both looked at each other, shaking their heads.

I said to the man from the office. "Any chance you know who it was?"

The man said, "It's self-entry. People come and go."

"But isn't there a way to know who it might've been?"

The man shook his head, looking at Collins and Helms as if he didn't know if he needed to answer me.

I looked inside the initial unit we looked at. "This was it," I said. "I'm sure of it now." I looked at the man from the office. "So you're saying these two aren't rented? You have nobody's name?"

He said, "That's correct."

Helms gave me a look, like he wasn't about to believe a word I was saying. "You playing some kind of game with us, Walsh?"

"Why would you say that?"

Detective Collins had her eyebrows raised, as if waiting for me to give some kind of explanation.

"I'm telling you the truth," I said. "This unit was full." I looked at the number. "Unit one-oh-one-seven. This is it." I turned to the storage man. "You must have employees, no?"

He nodded, but appeared confused why I'd ask.

I turned to Collins and Helms. "Shouldn't we talk to them?"

Helms said, "We?" He laughed. "There is no 'we.'"

I glanced at Collins, her eyes on the empty unit, like she was thinking. "Jesus Christ," she said under her breath, then started to walk away.

I said to the man, "Can we see a list of your employees?"

Detective Collins stopped and turned to me, her voice raised. "Walsh! That's enough. You're not a cop. Stop acting like one. If we need your help, we'll ask for it."

It looked to me like the young detective was more worried about me stepping on her toes than getting any answers. I was afraid at that point neither she nor Helms were going to believe much of what I'd said. I thought maybe they assumed I was doing something to protect Kathy.

Detective Collins said to me, "What about the other unit?"

"Inside," I said. "The next level."

I looked back and forth, then pointed toward the back of the building, in the direction of the stairs Kathy and I had used that morning.

The storage man said, "We can take the elevator."

With the big belly he was carrying, he didn't appear to be the type whose first choice would be to use stairs unless absolutely necessary. And considering he sounded out of breath just from walking around the building, I figured he'd likely made the best choice.

We all walked to the front of the building and followed the man to a set of automatic sliding doors, through a lobby, and up the elevator. We stepped off into the same damp hallway I'd been in earlier. One of the hanging lights flickered.

Helms said, "Are you going to tell me you don't know this unit number, either?"

I didn't answer, my eyes on the unit numbers as we walked down the hall.

I said to the man, "What's your security like in here? I saw the cameras... The one out back is busted."

Collins gave me another one of her looks, as if I wasn't allowed to ask any more questions.

The man continued walking ahead. "It's somewhat outdated, but we're having a new camera system installed."

I said, "So your cameras don't work?"

"Some do." He didn't add anything else to it.

I stopped when I was close to the unit, which I actually had remembered. It was unit 2132. "This is it," I said, stepping back from the door so the storage man could open it.

This time, there was a lock.

"Do you know who this unit belongs to?" Helms said.

The man shook his head, crouched down, and slid his master key into the lock. "I will have to look," he said. "But, if whoever has rented it paid cash, I don't always know if they're telling the truth about who they are."

"You don't check identification?" I said.

The man took the lock off and lifted the door. "You never know what is real and what is not," the man said, without giving me any further explanation.

I was happy to see the desk was still in the unit. "See that?" I said, as if proud of myself. "Go ahead, look in that drawer."

Detective Collins stepped between me and the storage guy, and into the unit. She knelt down at the desk and opened the drawer, reaching inside. She came out with a single piece of paper with tape on it, holding it up as she turned. "This is it," she said. "The drawer's empty."

Chapter 22

After a drive with more questions I wasn't able to answer, Detective Collins dropped me off at the entrance to my hotel. But right before I walked through the open door, she called out for me.

"Walsh?"

I looked back and she'd stepped out of her car, the door open, the engine still running.

I walked back toward her and she didn't speak right away, like she was thinking. "I hope you're not trying to hide something from us," she said.

I shook my head. "I don't know how many times I have to tell you," I said. "I have no reason to lie about any of this."

"I just hope you'd tell me if there's more to the story. I don't understand how those units could be emptied out like that, in such a short amount of time."

"Someone must've either followed us, or'd been watching us. All they'd need is a duffel bag, grab that money in five minutes and be long gone. The appliances and all those TVs, well..." I thought about the white box truck, but neither Helms or Collins seemed too concerned about it being there for some reason.

Collins said, "I know you're not going to like this, but it's hard for us not to believe there's something between you and Mrs. Arnold you're not telling us."

I waited before I responded. I thought maybe she was hoping I'd slip up, admit something I hadn't about me and Kathy. But there was nothing to tell. I knew she had a point, of course. It didn't look good. "I wish there was a way I could convince you, but I can't tell you what happened. I don't know."

Collins said, "What else did she say to you when she dropped you off at the hotel?"

"Do you think I'm going to change my answer from what I told you and Helms the last two times you asked me?"

Collins frowned. "Show me some respect," she said. "Just because I'm younger than you, doesn't mean—"

"Respect goes both ways," I said.

Collins glared at me, eyes narrowed, then turned and got back into her car.

I said, "Can I ask you a question?"

She pulled the car door closed but had the window open, looking up at me. "It depends," she said, with a playful look, as if all of a sudden we were buddies.

"Do you even have any real suspects?" I said.

Her surprised look, eyebrows raised, said *how dare you* as she stepped out of the car and stood in front of me, possibly holding herself back from throwing a punch. "What makes you think you know everything we're doing? You have no idea who we're looking at, what other suspects, we have, or—"

"I'm just asking a simple question," I said.

She glared back at me without a response.

I said, "I didn't think so."

Detective Collins swallowed hard before she turned and got back into her vehicle. "Your arrogance is going to get you in trouble," she said, climbing behind the wheel and slamming her door closed. But her window was down.

"What arrogance?" I said. "I'm just asking if you have any real leads. And you think that's arrogant?"

Collins shifted her car into drive and started to pull away, but jacked up when she slammed on her brakes. She looked at me out the window. "You think because I'm young, because I'm a woman, I don't know what I'm doing?"

"What?" I let out a laugh, but it was more of a nervous one than anything. Collins was visibly fuming, but I was somewhat surprised how easily I'd set her off. Before I could say another word, she hit the gas and took off from me, tires screeching across the lot and out onto Northwest Tenth.

· · · · ● · ● · · · ·

The first thing I did when I got into my room was sit on the bed and call Alex from the hotel phone.

There was barely a half ring when she answered. "Hello?"

"Hey," I said. "It's me."

"Henry? Where are you?" she said, a clear sound of concern in her voice.

"I'm sorry. I should have tried to call you, but—"

"You didn't answer me," she said. "Where are you?"

"Oh, sorry. At the hotel."

"No you're not," she said. "I was just there."

I stood up from the bed and looked toward the door. "What? You're at my hotel? Are you serious?"

She was quiet, and didn't answer. As tough as Alex was—tougher than most—I couldn't help but wonder why she wasn't answering.

"Alex?" I said.

There was a crack in her voice: "I... I thought something happened to you."

"I don't understand," I said. "You're here? At the hotel?"

"I'm actually... I was on my way to the police station. I didn't know what to do or who to call. Why didn't you answer your phone?"

I heard her question, but was trying to wrap my head around what was going on. "How far away are you?"

"From the hotel? I don't know. Maybe twenty minutes? Hold on," she said. "Let me pull over. I think I'm a couple miles from the police station."

I thought about how much time I'd spent out in the parking lot with Detective Collins. I knew I must've only missed Alex by a handful of minutes.

She said, "But why didn't you call me back? You wouldn't answer your phone... my texts. And when you didn't—"

"I'm sorry," I said. "My phone's dead."

....

I stood outside the lobby waiting, seeing a black Toyota Camry pull into the hotel parking lot with Alex behind the wheel. I watched her drive up and down both sides of the lot. There weren't any parking spaces available. She finally turned the corner and drove around to the back of the hotel.

I hurried after her, trying to ignore the pain that had returned in my leg.

Alex bounded out of the car and ran toward me, jumping into my arms. She kissed me, and I could feel wet from her tears against my cheek.

"I've never been so certain something bad happened to you," she said, holding me so tight, her arms wrapped around my neck, it was hard for me to breathe.

"Don't worry," I said, my voice strained. "Everything's okay."

I wasn't sure if that was true.

She looked at my face, touching the small cut under my eye. "What happened here?"

"Oh, uh... Kathy's husband attacked me."

"Why?"

We grabbed her bag from the rental car and I went ahead and gave her the rundown of most of what had happened, from the park to Kathy disappearing. It was all news to Alex.

We walked inside the hotel and she looked at my leg, the bandage covered by my pants. "Are you sure you don't need a doctor?"

I smiled, shaking my head. "I'm sorry you left Virginia," I said. "I hope your parents weren't too upset when you told them why you were leaving."

"I didn't tell Mom the whole story. But Dad... He was the one who called his friend, the one with the plane, got him to fly me down here."

The bag I carried for her was heavy, and I had a feeling it wasn't just clothes inside of it.

We walked across the lobby and stood at the elevator, waiting.

Alex said, "Don't you think it's more than just a coincidence Kathy disappeared at the same time those units got cleaned out?"

"I don't know what to think," I said. "I know the cops are suspicious. I'm not convinced they're even going all out to find her."

"They don't think she's really missing?" she said.

"Well, they're asking the same question you just did. And they know she was the one who took me there and showed me what was inside those storage units."

"But you don't think she would've faked her own disappearance?" she said.

The elevator door opened and we stepped inside. We rode it to the sixth floor without me giving Alex a straight answer to her question.

I didn't have one to give.

Once we were in the hotel room, Alex opened her backpack on the bed. She took out her computer and two guns.

She said, "The concerning thing to me is these two detectives seem to think you know more than you do," she said. "I assume you've been honest with them?"

I nodded. "I've told them everything. I don't want them to have a chance to pin anything on me."

Alex picked up one of the guns, looking at me like she didn't know what to say. "Don't you think if we find who took that money, we'll find Brock's killer?"

"I don't know," I said. "But a moment ago you suggested Kathy could be the one who emptied out those storage units."

"I was just asking," she said, staring back at me with her eyes somewhat squinted. "Why do you seem like you've been defending her?"

"I'm not," I said. "I already told you I let the cops know everything."

"But not about what happened in the park?" she said.

I shook my head. "I didn't have much reason to hold that back. I'm not even sure why I did."

"Because you're afraid Kathy had something to do with you being attacked there?"

"What?" I shook my head. "I'm telling you the truth. I don't know why I didn't tell them. I'm still surprised I haven't heard anything about it."

Alex said, "What about the husband? You said he attacked you. I assume the cops questioned him about his wife's disappearance?"

"I don't know," I said. "They're not telling me much about any of it. I asked if they had any other suspects."

"And what did you get from it?" she said.

"Nothing at all. Detective Collins said I was arrogant."

Chapter 23

The first thing we did after we left the hotel was replace my phone, which turned out to be more of an expense than I'd bargained for. I wasn't one for having the fanciest phone, or the fanciest of anything. But the price tag shocked me, and made me wonder if I'd be better off without it.

Living without a phone—and maybe entirely off the grid—was something that had honestly gone through my mind, more than once.

The truth was, it wasn't actually an option. Not unless I was in another business; one where nobody was ever looking for me.

Alex had a much better grip on technology than I did, and wouldn't let me go for the cheapest option. That meant the new phone set me back over four hundred dollars.

The kid behind the counter was able to somehow get my new phone set up for me, with all of my contacts and everything else I needed transferred from the old phone, even though it was dead.

And as soon as I stepped outside the store, it didn't take more than a few seconds for the new phone to start chirping and buzzing. All the calls and messages I'd missed started coming through.

By the time Alex and I made it to her car, I had nearly twenty text messages missed, seventeen missed calls, and eight messages. Plenty of the messages were from Alex, but then I saw one from Kathy. I listened, and it was as if she didn't know if she was talking to my voicemail or if it was actually me on the other end:

"Henry? Are you there? There's a..."

Her voice cracked and dropped out from what sounded like a weak phone signal. I couldn't make out her words until her voice said:

"He's following me."

That was the last thing I heard on her message. I glanced at the phone, but the next message had already started again. It was garbled background noise, but I could still hear somebody talking. But then it stopped and the call disconnected.

Alex was already in the rental car, the engine running with the cool air blowing out from inside when I opened the passenger-side door.

"Listen," I said, and replayed the first message on speaker.

We both sat in silence, Kathy's voice nervously coming through the phone:

"He's following me."

Alex looked at me, eyes wide.

"Could be anyone," I said.

Alex said, "What about the husband?"

"You think he kidnapped his wife?"

"No, I mean... What else did he say?"

"To me? He mostly let his fists do the talking."

"Didn't he say why he went after you?" she said.

I had to think about it. "He thought I had something to do with it."

We were both quiet, the cold air blowing from the vents, radio off, engine running.

"Why?" she said. "She must've told him something to make him believe you were caught up in everything."

"I'm not sure he knows much of anything," I said. "But it's hard to know for sure."

I looked at my phone and flipped through the other messages. There was another call from a local number, so I tapped the button and listened:

Uh, hello sir, this is Ken Hardy from Hardy's Auto Body. Your BMW is ready to be picked up.

"I need to pick up Billy's car," I said, glancing at the clock on the dashboard.

Alex said, "You don't think we should talk to Kathy's husband?" She turned her phone to me with GPS already pulled up. "His business is ten minutes from here."

I thought for a moment. "I'm just not sure he's interested in talking to me."

"Don't you think he wants all the help he can get, finding his wife?"

"You would think so," I said, shaking my head. "But not from me."

But Alex had a look on her face, like she had something else in mind.

"What are you thinking?" I said.

She shrugged. "You just have to wonder about this guy, the way he reacted toward you, coming after you the way he did. You think it might've been an act? Like he was covering something up?"

I toyed around with it in my head. "I'm just not sure," I said. "Anything's possible, the way this has all been going."

....

Alex turned down Industrial Park Lane and stopped at the sign listing the commercial tenants, where the logo and name, Arnold Cleaning Services, Inc., was up top and larger than the others.

We continued ahead and turned in when we saw nine vans parked around the side of the brick building where three garage doors were wide open, eight men and three women hanging around outside talking, some laughing, all dressed in the same blue uniforms. Some were sipping from travel mugs while others looked to be working hard, pushing machines onto ramps sticking out the back of some of the vans.

But they all stopped when we drove closer to the building.

Alex said, "Do you recognize anyone?"

I looked at them all, tried to get a decent look at each, but most had gone back to whatever they were doing. Only one stood still, watching us until we stopped.

He turned and went inside through one of the open garage doors.

Alex parked and we both got out and walked toward the workers.

It was mostly quiet outside, although there was loud, heavy banging echoing somewhere in the distance. I watched a truck raising a commercial dumpster, emptying garbage into the back.

Two younger men in the blue uniforms walked toward one of the vans, one with a plastic jug in his hand. He stood at the back of the vehicle.

I said, "Hey, Luke Arnold around?"

"Mr. Arnold?" the young man said. He nodded toward the garage doors. "Should be in his office."

"Any chance you could tell him Henry Walsh is outside, and would like to talk to him?"

He looked from me to Alex, like he was hesitating.

Alex, her voice low, leaned into me. "Can't we just go inside?"

I said, "If he's going to act the way he did when I first saw him, I'd rather it be out here."

The man opened the doors on the back of his van and placed the gallon jug inside, slamming the doors closed with a loud bang.

I couldn't tell if the man was ignoring us, or deciding what to do.

I said, "Would you mind checking? I'm sure he'd be happy to hear I'm out here."

The man paused, the driver-side door open. He said to the other young man, already in the driver seat, "Gimme a minute." He went into the garage and disappeared inside.

The garbage truck that had emptied the dumpster drove in our direction, and I looked at the driver behind the wheel, until he started to pass. The door had a Canzano Waste Management logo on the side of it.

I said to Alex. "You see that? Canzano."

"Didn't you talk to him?" she said.

I paused to think about it, then shook my head. "Detective Collins said they have no reason to believe he had any kind of involvement."

Alex had her eyes on the garbage truck, pulling out of the parking lot. It turned right onto the main road and continued through the industrial park until we couldn't see the truck anymore.

The young man who'd gone inside came out from the garage, but he didn't say a word to us, continuing toward the van. He climbed inside and started the engine.

"Hey," I said, loud enough I thought he could hear me, even with the window up. I walked toward him, but the young man acted as if I wasn't there and drove away without saying a word.

I started for the open garage, Alex following. But before I got close to it, two men much bigger and wider than me stepped outside and stood, arms crossed, shoulder to shoulder blocking our path.

One of the two, in a voice so deep it was almost hard to hear, said, "It'd be in your best interest to leave this facility."

Both just stared at me and Alex.

I said. "You know, your boss sure has a way of making it pretty clear he's got something to hide, doesn't he?" I tried to look past the two enormous creatures and into the garage. I could see some of the other uniformed men, looking our way.

A police vehicle turned off the road, coming toward us. I looked at Alex, then said to the two goons, "Is he serious? He called the cops?"

The Miami-Dade police vehicle continued toward us, then stopped next to Alex's rental.

A tall, skinny officer stepped out and looked inside the Toyota on his way over to us.

The two goons still hadn't moved. "Good morning, officer," one of them said.

The cop put his hand out, "Can I see some ID?"

Alex and I both looked at each other. It crossed my mind to refuse. But it wouldn't get us anywhere.

"Have we done something wrong?" Alex said. "All we did was get out of our car..." She nodded toward the Toyota. "That's my rental right there."

The skinny cop said, "We received a phone call; someone was trespassing."

"Trespassing?" I said, turning to the two goons. "Seriously?" I said to the officer, "We came here to talk to Mr. Arnold. I can't see how we're doing anything illegal."

"Well, this is private property," the cop said.

The two goons walked away, going inside the garage and disappearing through a doorway.

Alex and I decided to play the game, and handed the man our driver's licenses. "I don't know if you know who I am," I said, "but—"

The cop didn't answer, glancing at Alex's ID, handing it back to her, then looking at mine. "Henry Walsh? You're the private investigator, down here sticking your nose where it don't belong. Is that right?"

"The part about my nose isn't exactly accurate," I said. "I'm a licensed private investigator. Not just some hack trying to get in the way. And Mr. Arnold's wife is a friend of mine. I'm just as interested as anyone in making sure she's found... Alive."

The cop handed me back my license.

I said, "So, what now? You'll arrest us if we don't leave?"

The officer took a step forward. "If that's what you'd like…"

I could see on Alex's face she'd hoped I'd just shut my mouth. "Kind of a silly question," I said. "Isn't it?"

The cop's finger got awfully close to his taser, holstered on his belt.

"Whoa… relax," I said. "I'm telling you, we're not here to cause anyone any trouble."

The cop said, "Then I suggest you get in that car over there and hit the road. Or trouble's exactly what you'll find."

Alex pulled at my arm, but I resisted for a moment, until I finally realized even if the cop hadn't shown up, Luke Arnold wasn't going to talk to me.

I also realized I was probably better off dealing with what seemed like a levelheaded cop, versus the two goons Arnold sent out for me.

The officer stood still, waiting, his gaze fixed on mine, like a challenge, maybe hoping I'd push back just so he'd have something to do.

I put my hands up. "All right, all right. We're leaving."

Alex and I both got in her car.

"I don't get it," I said. "What's this guy got against me? Other than he's got something to hide?"

Alex started the engine and turned the car around, tires spinning on top of the asphalt. "It seems like the cops don't want you around, either," she said. "What else did that detective say last night?"

"Besides telling me I'm arrogant?"

Alex smiled, her eyes on the road.

"What?" I said. "I'm not arrogant. Am I?"

She looked in her rearview mirror, then gave me another glance and shook her head. "Anyone who knows you, knows you're not. But I'd be lying if I said you might not come off that way to someone who doesn't know you."

I folded my arms, thinking about it a little more.

"Arrogant?" I said, as if she misheard what I'd said.

Alex shook her head. "I didn't say you were. But... You're one of those people, where it might take someone a little time to figure out you've got a big heart." She smiled, eyes in the rearview mirror.

I looked out the back, saw the cop's car was behind us, but turned off down another road.

"This detective, Detective Collins," I said. "She's young. She's got no interest in hearing from someone who's been around the block."

Alex nodded like she understood, but didn't say much else about it, like she didn't want to get into the discussion about me rubbing someone the wrong way.

It wasn't the first time I had.

Alex turned into a place called Mugs Coffee and Donuts.

"What are we doing? Hoping to run into more cops?" I said.

Alex didn't laugh, turning off the car. "What else do you know about this guy?"

"Who? Luke Arnold?"

Alex nodded.

"It sounds like he's done well for himself with that cleaning business. He's older than her. And I know for a fact his punch is like the kick of a mule."

"You think he knows the cops?" she said.

"Looks that way, doesn't it?"

"What about Canzano? That truck was there today, so at the very least they have some kind of business relationship. But you don't even know if he knows Mr. Canzano, personally?"

"I don't," I said.

"What about Kathy?" she said. "Do she and Canzano know each other?"

"I don't know," I said. "But we should ask him."

"I'm surprised you haven't already," Alex said.

She was right, and I wasn't sure why I hadn't.

I said, "You know that guy I told you about? The writer from the *Miami Post*?"

Alex nodded. "The one from the restaurant where Steve Rogers was killed?"

"Exactly. I was thinking I should get in touch with him. He knows people, including Canzano. I just feel like it might be worth talking to him."

Alex shrugged, then nodded. "Why not? Do you know where he lives?"

"By the ballpark," I said. "Marlins Park."

Alex had her phone out, tapping the screen.

I rubbed the back of my neck, the sweat already soaking through the collar of my shirt.

"Can we go inside?" I said.

Alex looked up from her phone. "Oh, yeah. Sorry." She pushed open the driver-side door and we both got out.

I reached for the door at the entrance and Alex stepped past me. But before I went in after her, I stopped and looked back toward the street.

A Miami-Dade police vehicle was driving by, slowly, but sped up and took off as soon as I turned.

Alex was already at the counter when I walked up to her. "Hey," I said. "A cop just went by."

She looked toward the door. "The same one?"

"I don't know," I said. "He was out on the street. But whoever it was took off."

Chapter 24

ALEX DROPPED ME OFF at Hardy's Auto Body to pick up Billy's BMW, then met me back at the hotel where we left her car in the lot, since the police were now well aware of what we were driving.

The BMW looked good, and in even better shape than before the accident. It had a brand new paint job, two new wheels and, of course, all the broken windows replaced.

Even with my insurance covering a good chunk of the nut, the out-of-pocket expenses I'd incurred made my trip to Miami a costly one. In more ways than one.

We drove in on Northwest Seventh, past Marlins Park, the lights on over the ballpark, although there wasn't a game being played. We continued toward the high-rise apartment building straight ahead of us. I continued two blocks and turned into the parking lot under the building.

It was fairly bright in the lot, with more cars than I'd expected. It seemed to be full, but I noticed a handful of empty spaces on the far end of the lot, with VISITORS painted in white on the concrete.

I turned off the engine and sat for a moment, looked at my watch and turned to Alex. "I wish I hadn't dragged you into this."

"You didn't drag me into anything," she said. "I'm here because you can't do this alone." Alex pushed open the passenger door. "Let's go see if your new friend can get us some answers."

I don't think either one of us had much confidence he would. Just because Mr. Sheldon wrote about the crime scene in Florida didn't mean he was still in the trenches, or knew more than what he'd already told me the night Steve Rogers was killed... which was very little.

We walked past an older-model convertible Mercedes with forest-green paint, parked near the elevator. I remembered seeing it in the parking lot at the restaurant, but didn't think much of it at the time. My guess was it belonged to Sheldon.

Alex and I stepped in front of the elevator door, but when I pressed the button to go up, nothing happened.

Alex said, "You need a code." She pointed to the metal box on the white cinder-block wall.

"Great," I said, and looked around the lot, as if someone would show up and let us onto the elevator. "There's gotta be a lobby." I started toward the entrance where we drove into the lot.

Alex walked up behind me, her cell phone in her hand, glancing at the screen. "I found a phone number for a Joe Sheldon," she said, turning the screen so I could see it.

I said, "He told me he was in some kind of investigative business, but didn't get into the details. I'm not sure if that's his or not."

We walked on the sidewalk along the building, Alex with the phone to her ear.

It was getting late, and the air had cooled enough to where it was a little more comfortable, although a normal person would still consider the heat too much.

We turned the corner and stood at the front of the building. "He's not answering," she said. "And no voicemail. It just stopped ringing."

I pulled on the plate-glass door but, like the elevator, there was a keypad next to it.

That's when Alex's phone rang, and she looked at the screen. "It's the number I just called." She answered, "Hello?"

I watched her nod, then smile. "Yeah, that was me who called. My name's Alex. Alex Jepson. I'm down here with... Hang on. Someone wants to talk to you."

I took the phone from her. "Hello? Joe?"

The male voice on the other end said, "Hey man, what can I do you for? You just called?"

"Yes, that was me. We're downstairs, outside the lobby of your apartment building."

There was a pause on the other end. I could hear music playing in the background. "I'm sorry," he said. "But who did you say this is again?"

"Oh, I actually didn't. It's Henry Walsh. We met that night at that place, Mickey Cho's? The night the man was stabbed at the bar."

"Ooohhh yeaaahh. The private dick, right?"

I couldn't remember the last time I'd been called that. "Yes, you got it."

Joe said, "Did you say you're in my building?"

"No, not exactly. We're outside the lobby. I was hoping we could talk to you about—"

"Who's 'we?'" Joe said.

"Uh, just me and my, uh... my partner, Alex. The one who answered the phone."

The music was still loud coming through the phone, but Joe didn't say anything for a moment or two.

I said, "Joe? You there?"

"I'm here. Yeah. I just... What is it I can help you with?"

"Well, I was hoping you could come down here. Or, if we could come up..."

"Oh, okay. Yeah, sure, man. Hang tight. I got it," he said.

A few seconds later the door buzzed and I grabbed it right away, before it locked on us.

· · · • · • • • · ·

Elvis Costello's "Every Day I Write the Book" was playing when we entered the apartment, Joe standing at the door with the same kind of red drink in his hand he had at the restaurant the night Steve Rogers was killed.

"Henry," I said, shaking Joe's hand.

But his eyes went right to Alex, a slight smile on his face as he reached out his hand for hers. "Joe Sheldon."

"Alex."

I spotted a bottle of Smirnoff on the counter with a small wood cutting board with a knife and cut-up pieces of lime on top of it.

"Either of you want a drink?" he said, walking along the wall of record albums, lowering the volume on the music. He raised his glass. "I make a good vodka cranberry."

I wasn't sure what'd make it good, or different from any other vodka mixed with cranberry. Pretty straightforward.

Alex and I both refused the drink.

The music was apparently coming from an old stereo system and turntable placed on what looked like painted DIY shelves running from one end of the wall to the other. On either side of the stereo centered on the top shelf were hundreds, maybe even thousands of records.

Two big wooden speakers, the kind I hadn't seen in decades, sat in opposite corners of the apartment, each speaker at least four feet high and a foot or so wide with the wood sides and black foam face. Some kind of plant or ivy hung down to the hardwood floor from a pot on top of the speaker near the sliding glass door.

Joe Sheldon, no doubt, was old-school. Even his furniture appeared to be from another time. Not exactly antiques, but more eighties, nineties. Vintage.

Joe had a laptop open on the table in his kitchen; he closed the lid and placed it on the counter. "Have a seat," he said. He took a sip of his drink and sat at one end of the table. "So, you two... Are you a couple? Or—"

"Business partners," Alex said, without hesitation.

Joe smiled, looking from me to Alex, like he didn't believe her. He said, "You're both from Jacksonville, uh?"

"We live in Fernandina Beach. Got an office in Jacksonville," I said. "I grew up in Fernandina Beach, and we recently moved there again."

Joe said, "We?" He smiled. "I thought so. I can see it in your faces... You're not just business partners."

I wasn't sure why it mattered to him, other than asking questions was engrained in him, maybe from his background as a journalist. Maybe it was just in the blood.

"We're looking for Kathy Arnold," I said.

Joe folded his arms, the look on his face turning serious. "Kathy Arnold?"

"Brock Mason's sister. You remember, we talked about Brock the other night?"

"Oh, right. Yeah," he said. "I did hear about that. I guess it wasn't clear what happened, from what I hear. They don't know if she'd been abducted or decided to take off?"

"That's certainly a question that's out there," I said.

Joe was about to take a sip of his drink, but slowly lowered the glass back to the table. "This have something to do with the guy who was stabbed at Mickey Cho's?"

I looked across the table at Alex, then nodded. "Mason was mixed up in something before he was killed. I'm just not sure what it was."

"The sister too?" Joe said.

"I'm not sure about her either. I know Brock and his girl-friend were up to something, may've gotten in over their heads. Maybe crossed the wrong person, along the way."

"In what way?" Joe said.

I explained as much as I could to him, including what Kathy had shown me at Save-More Storage. "The more I think about it," I said, "The more I think it's possible she'd hoped I'd help her."

"Do what? Get the money out of there?" Joe said.

"Something along those lines," I said.

Joe pulled at his chin. "So, you think maybe these three stole from someone who didn't take too kindly to it?" Joe said.

"I wish I could answer that," I said. "But it seems that way."

Joe had a confused look on his face, like he was thinking it all through. He said, "So, what's this got to do with me?"

Elvis Costello's "Oliver's Army" played in the adjacent room, the volume low now.

"I guess I'm just hoping since you knew a bit about Brock Mason and that scheme he was wrapped up in, maybe you know some of the people he's gotten involved with over the years. To be honest, I don't even know where to turn right now. The cops don't want me involved, and part of it might be because they think I know more than I do."

Joe took his time, his eyes on his drink, wheels turning. "Listen," he said. "Don't take this the wrong way, but I'm not exactly sure I want to be wrapped up in any of whatever's going on here." He stuck his finger in the glass, touching the lime floating on top of the ice, then raised his gaze. "See, the thing is, I gotta lay low. I think I mentioned to you, I've got this gig..."

"Some kind of investigative work," I said nodding. "Isn't that what you said?"

"Well, yeah. You could call it that. But, well, let's just say whatever it is... It's paying my bills right now. I can't afford getting my name out there. I guess I don't need the attention, if you know what I mean?"

"Of course," I said. "I'm not asking you to get involved. I'm just hoping maybe you can point me in some kind of direction, maybe know someone I could talk to?"

Alex was looking at me, the expression on her face like she was wondering why we were even there.

Joe didn't seem to know much of anything.

He said, "Well, what about the sister? No idea where she might've gone?"

I shook my head. "I'm starting to think that's the way she wants it."

Joe said, "She's married, right?"

"Kathy?" I nodded, "Yeah. To a guy named Luke Arnold. Owns a commercial cleaning business, here in Miami."

Joe took a drink, eyes somewhat squinted as he leaned back in his chair, his hand on the glass on the table. "Is he involved with Ray Canzano by any chance?"

"I don't know if he's involved with him. But I stopped over there, at Arnold's place of business, and saw a Canzano truck emptying out a dumpster. Can't say much else about it, or if it means much of anything at all." I paused, glancing at Alex, then said, "Why?"

Joe shrugged. "Just asking. Cleaning business. Garbage business. Kind of could go hand in hand, but I'm just asking. I assume you've talked to Canzano already?"

"Well, not exactly," I said.

Alex said to Joe, "What about the name Vincent Giotti?"

Joe didn't hesitate a second. "Vincent? Yeah, I actually know, well, I *knew* him personally years back, when we were both younger."

"Wasn't he the only other person who did time with Brock?" Alex said.

"He was the one in charge of the nonprofit. But, if what you're asking is if he somehow had something to do with your friend getting killed, or Kathy Arnold…"

"I'm just wondering," Alex said. "I couldn't find any direct ties, but he seemed to be tightly connected to some well-known Mob names down here."

Joe said, "Vin Giotti's not involved in anything anymore. He had a stroke while he was still in prison. Been in a coma ever since, up in Fort Lauderdale. Hasn't even opened an eye in over a year."

Alex and I looked at each other, and I guessed she wondered how neither of us had found anything about it online.

"They kept it quiet," Joe said, as if he knew what we were thinking. "Never made it in the paper."

The three of us were quiet. Even the music had stopped playing.

Joe got up and went into the other room. I leaned back and saw him changing out the record on his turntable. He walked back over as the music started to play. He'd put on James Taylor, "Sweet Baby James."

"You like James Taylor?" he said, grabbing his glass to make another drink.

Alex and I both nodded.

Joe said, "You sure neither of you want a drink?" He pulled the cranberry juice from the refrigerator and poured it over his vodka, then sat back down. "I would talk to Canzano. But, be careful," he said. "He's kind of a hothead. Also has guys working for him you won't want to mess with." He sipped his drink. "Word is he's also got cops on his payroll."

"Is that a fact?" I said.

Joe shrugged. "Just what I'd heard. But, what I'd take from it is you might want to be careful."

Chapter 25

I WAS BEHIND THE wheel of the BMW, music on the radio on the way to Raymond Canzano's house in Coral Gables, a city southwest of Miami. Alex had yawned a couple of times in the passenger seat and had been more quiet than usual.

"Are you going to make it?" I said. "I can take you back to the hotel, if you want to get some sleep?"

Alex straightened up in the seat. "No, I'm okay."

I had a feeling Alex had started to believe it was true that Kathy had pulled this off on her own—or with someone's help—to only make it appear she was missing.

But I couldn't assume that was the case. Not if it turned out something bad happened to Kathy.

We drove another mile, when I saw the 7-Eleven up ahead. I glanced at the needle on the gas gauge. "We need to get some gas." Continuing on Southwest Eighth, I turned into the 7-Eleven parking lot and pulled up to one of the pumps.

I got out and looked toward the quiet street when a car drove by and stopped a few feet past the gas station's entrance, but then took off.

I slid the nozzle into the tank and watched the car turn into the parking lot of the building right after the 7-Eleven.

The lights from the vehicle shined through the wooden privacy fence between the two buildings from on the other side.

Alex stepped out of the car and stretched her arms and looked my way. "Are you all right?" She followed my eyes to the sliver of light coming through the fence.

"That car over there, on the other side of the fence... It drove by, stopped out in the street, then pulled ahead and into that lot."

Alex looked toward the fence, then at me, as if she didn't know what to say.

"Maybe it's nothing," I said, putting enough gas into the tank to get us through the night. I finished up and got back in the car. As soon as Alex got in we took off for the street, then turned into the lot where the car was parked.

But the car wasn't there.

"Are you sure it was a car?" Alex said.

"Yeah, I'm sure. Didn't you see the headlights coming through the fence?"

"All I saw were lights," she said, leaning forward and looking up through the windshield at the bright light, high up on a pole in the parking lot. "You sure it wasn't from that?"

But before I answered, a car drove out from the other side of the building and took off onto the street.

I turned the BMW around and drove after the car. I didn't think I should overreact, and go speeding after it. But I didn't want whoever it was to get too far ahead, either.

"Why are you following that car?" she said. "It was probably a couple of high school kids making out or something."

It may not have mattered at that point, because I couldn't see the car anywhere. But I continued driving in the same direction, going past the buildings on Tamiami Trail. I started to speed up, a feeling in my gut telling me it was more than just some random person parking in the middle of the night. But I had to practically slam on my brakes when the traffic lights at Southwest Forty-Ninth turned red.

I said, "You really think they would've taken off like that if they didn't know we were pulling in that lot?"

Alex appeared skeptical. "I'm sure it was nothing," she said. "Did you even see what kind of car it was?"

"Looked like a dark, older sedan," I said. "But, no, I didn't get a good look."

· · • · • · · · ·

The lights were on inside the Canzano home and, with it being dark outside other than the glow from the streetlights, I could see in through the windows where a woman—Mrs. Canzano, I presumed—paced back and forth, a phone to her ear.

She appeared animated, throwing her hands up as she spoke.

"Maybe you should wait here," I said, stepping out of the car. "Just in case."

Alex had already opened the passenger-side door, but pulled it closed. "Be careful," she said.

I headed for the house, the only sound outside in the quiet suburban neighborhood being the katydids and air-conditioning units kicking on and off randomly, outside the various houses.

I went up the steps and knocked on the front door, turning to the street when I heard a vehicle, but it continued past the house without slowing or stopping.

The door opened behind me and I turned to a woman, dressed in what looked like pajama shorts and a T-shirt top, looking me up and down. "Yes?"

"Mrs. Canzano?"

She had one hand behind her back. I couldn't help but wonder what she was holding.

I made sure she could see my hands, and that I was unarmed. "My name's Henry Walsh. I'm sorry, but I really need to talk to your husband."

"Raymond?" she said, shaking her head. "He's not here."

I tried to look past her, into the house. I could hear music playing, and saw a television on. "Do you know where I can find him?"

"He tells me he's at work. He likes to go in late at night. At least that's what he says, even when I know it's not the truth." She looked out at the street where I'd parked the Beemer.

I glanced back too, to be able to see Alex sitting in the car. But it had gotten dark enough out and I'd parked in the shadows of the trees, and it was impossible to see anyone inside.

"Do you mind telling me what you want with my husband?"

I handed her my business card. "I'm a private investigator."

"Oh," she said, with a swallow she tried to hide.

A phone rang inside the house and Mrs. Canzano pushed open the door and left it wide open as she stepped inside.

I stayed outside, but peered in, watching her pick up the phone. "Hello?" I was right to worry about her hand behind her back, seeing her place a small .38 on the table with the phone.

She glanced at me and said into the phone, "Oh hello, dear. Speak of the devil." She listened, nodding. "There's a man here..." She looked at my business card in her hand. "His name's Henry Walsh. A private investigator." She glanced over at me and winked, like she was doing me a favor. Maybe she was. She then covered the phone with her hand and looked out the door at me. "He wants to know what you want."

I was hesitant to say, at first, but then knew it didn't matter much whether he knew now or later. I said, "Tell him it's about Brock Mason."

She put the phone back to her ear, and I could see on her face she appeared to be thinking something through, before she opened her mouth. There was no doubt a look of concern on her face. "It's about Brock Mason," she said.

I wasn't sure I heard her right, watching Mrs. Canzano hold the phone a few inches from her ear, her eyes squinted. I could actually hear her husband's loud voice coming through the phone.

"Okay, dear. Stop yelling please."

I poked my head inside the door. "Tell him it's important we talk."

She raised her eyebrows with a look on her face like I'd said something foolish. She said into the phone, "Mr. Walsh said it's important that you talk. Maybe you can meet him?" She pulled the phone from her ear as she had a moment ago, her eyes almost squeezed closed. "All right, all right. I can't even understand you when you yell like that." She listened, nodding. "All right, hon. I'll tell him." She hung the phone up and said to me, "My husband said you have thirty seconds to get out, or somebody will be here to take you out."

She walked over to the door, as if she was about to close it on me.

"Wait," I said, my hand out so she couldn't. "Can you tell me where he is?"

Mrs. Canzano sighed, rolling her eyes. "You're the private investigator. Figure it out." She slammed the door closed and turned off the exterior light over my head.

Chapter 26

I PULLED UP TO the gate at Canzano Waste Management, the entire property enclosed by a ten-foot-high chain-link fence with barbed wire across the top. There were at least twenty or more yellow garbage trucks parked along the building on the other side, with Canzano Waste Management painted on each one.

"How are we supposed to get in there?" Alex said, looking ahead through the windshield, pointing. "See those cameras?"

I glanced at the one camera over the entrance gate and got out of the car, waving my arms.

Alex got out from the passenger side. "What are you doing?"

"If Canzano's here, he'll see me out here. Or, at least someone will."

"It doesn't even look like there's anyone here," Alex said, her voice hushed.

But I heard a sound and looked at the building in the distance. A door had opened, and someone was walking through the dark shadows toward us.

"See?" I said to Alex. "It worked."

The man got closer and I could see he was a security guard, older with his white hair buzzed short. He stood on the other side of the fence looking from me to Alex, hand on his holster. "Is there something I can do for you?"

"I'm looking for Raymond Canzano," I said.

The man paused, then walked over to the small, brick, guard's building and pressed a button. The gate started to slide open. "Leave the vehicle out here," he said, looking me up and down. "You armed?" he said, patting me down.

"No."

He turned to Alex and leaned over, started to pat her down but she slapped his hand. "I don't have a gun," she said, giving him a look that'd cause any man to think twice.

"How am I supposed to know?" the guard said.

Alex looked into his eyes. "Because I just told you. I don't even like guns."

The guard gave a tight-lipped grin and stepped back from Alex, nodding. "All right," he said, and started through the gate.

I was actually surprised there wasn't much persuading involved to get the guard to let us in. I could only guess Canzano was waiting for us.

We went through the gate and the guard hit a button to close it behind us. He walked ahead at a good pace, long steps. His posture was military-like, and I had a feeling he wasn't your everyday security guard.

We continued until we were at the same door at the building he'd first come out of, using a key from a ring he had on his belt to unlock it.

He stepped inside a narrow hall with what looked like storage rooms on either side. A light came from farther down the hall, but it was somewhat dim. Another light came through a doorway to our right, and as we continued past it I noticed six or so monitors up on the wall in front of a desk and chair. One of the monitors showed the exterior and the entrance, with the BMW parked outside the gate.

The guard had already walked ahead of us while I continued to glance from one monitor to the other, and stopped cold when I saw an exterior shot of a dimly lit area outside with another building with three garage doors. A white box truck was parked in front of it.

The security guard came through the door and said, "Let's go! Get out of here!"

I ignored him and pointed at the monitor. "Where's this truck?"

The man tried to grab my arm, but I ripped it from his grasp and gave him a shove, pushing him against the wall.

A man yelled from outside the room. "Hey! Back off!"

I looked through the doorway and there was a man holding Alex from behind, with a gun pointed right at me. "You all right, Mike?" he said.

I let go of the security guard—named Mike, apparently—and he gave me a shove as he straightened, then pulled his gun and pressed it into my back.

"You must be Ray," I said, looking at the man in the hall.

"Raymond," he said, correcting me.

Canzano was older looking than I'd expected—white hair, or what was left of it, and much heavier than the pictures we saw online. He wore a tight black T-shirt barely covering his big stomach, his big upper body squeezed into it like sausage meat.

Canzano lowered the gun and let go of Alex. "Let's all just relax," he said. "All right?"

"I want to know what's in that truck," I said.

Canzano shrugged. "What truck?"

"We don't need to play games," I said, turning and pointing at the monitor. "That truck. I should've known it was you."

Canzano stepped past me and clicked a button in front of the monitor with the truck. The screen went black after he apparently turned off the camera. "I don't know what you're talking about."

"Then show me the truck," I said. "If you have nothing to hide."

Canzano smiled, almost rolling his eyes. "You want to see the truck?" He gave the security guard a nod. "We can show him the truck, right, Mike?"

Mike didn't respond, but had his gun out, holding it low and pointed at me.

"Do you really need that?" I said, asking about the gun.

Canzano said to Mike, "You can put it away." He smiled at me and Alex with a crooked grin. "Assuming, moving forward, we can all behave like adults?"

"You always work this late into the night?" I said.

Canzano walked ahead of us, looking back over his shoulder at me. "I work all the time. Keeps me out of the house. You know what I mean?"

He walked through another door and turned on the lights in a large, factory-like area with dozens of long machines at least twenty feet long and maybe ten feet high. There was a strong odor, a mix of burning plastic and garbage.

"What is this place?" I said.

"Sorting and recycling equipment," Canzano said. "That's where the money's at today."

"Oh, I thought maybe it was stealing appliances," I said.

Canzano glared at me, then continued ahead without a response.

Alex and I followed and I gave her a quick look to make sure she was okay.

She'd been quiet, and had a worried look on her face.

We exited the recycling area and headed down another hall until Canzano stopped at another steel door. He turned the lock and pushed it open, and we were outside.

The white box truck was parked by a steel building with garage doors on the front of it. I said, "I saw this truck at Save-More Storage."

Canzano had a cocky, sly smile on his face.

"Was it you?" I said.

Canzano didn't answer, stopping at the back of the truck. He nodded toward the security guard standing behind me. "You got the key?"

The guard nodded and stepped past him, pulled the keys from his belt and picked through the dozen or so on the ring. He slid one into the lock on the box truck's rear door. He lifted it, and used the flashlight from his belt to show us the inside.

But the back of the truck was empty.

"This doesn't show me anything," I said. "Obviously, you emptied it out."

"You don't know what you're talking about," Canzano said.

But I noticed something on the floor, toward the front of the cargo area, and climbed up inside.

"Hey, what do you think you're doing?" Canzano said.

I glanced back as he nudged the security guard to follow me.

Canzano said, "Get him down from there. here."

I leaned over and picked up what looked like some kind of label with Magic City Appliances on it. Just as I turned, the security guard was in the truck and standing behind me.

He ripped the label from my hand, then swung his gun and hit me in the head with it.

Alex yelled, "Henry!"

I dropped to the truck's floor on one knee, holding the side of my head where I'd been hit. But I came up fast and drove my shoulder into the security guard's mid-section, sending him straight out the back of the truck and onto the pavement.

He laid on his back, groaning in pain as I jumped down after him.

"Jesus Christ," Canzano said. He had his gun out, but kept it down by his side.

I held my hands up in front of me. "Sorry about that," I said.

Canzano let out a sigh, shaking his head as he reached out and helped his security guard to his feet.

The man appeared to be fine.

"Magic City Appliance?" I said.

Canzano's eyebrows raised. "What about it?"

"I saw the label." I looked at the ground where I'd fallen from the truck with the security guard, and saw he'd dropped it. "Here," I said, bending down to pick it up.

Canzano shrugged. "So?"

"I saw what was in that storage unit. And I saw this truck leaving."

Canzano still wasn't responding, instead giving me this stupid look, like he'd already decided the best thing he could do was play dumb.

I said, "Admit it. You emptied out those storage units."

He ripped the label from my hand and stuck it in his pocket. "What storage unit?"

I looked toward the metal building a few feet from where we stood, no windows on the outside, from what I could see. "Why don't you show me what's inside that building?"

Canzano said, "What is it you want from me? What's it matter to you who stole what from where?"

"Did you kill Brock and Jillian?" I said. "Were you afraid they'd rat you out?"

"Rat me out?" Canzano kept it up. "For what? I haven't done nothing wrong. I don't know anything about this storage unit you speak of."

I didn't know how many years he'd been in Florida, but I did know the old saying: *You can take the man out of New York, but you can't take New York out of the man.*

I said, "I saw the appliances, the TVs... The drawer full of cash."

Canzano's eyes opened wide. "Cash?" His eyes widened as if surprised. He glanced at the guard but Mike just shrugged. Canzano said to me, "You found the... You found cash in the storage unit? How much are we talkin'?"

I couldn't figure out if this guy was pulling my leg. "You expect me to believe you didn't take that cash?"

Canzano shook his head and raised his gun. "Where is it?" he said.

"Where is what?" I said. "The money?"

Canzano took a step closer to me, his gun pointed at my face, teeth gnashed. "Where is it?"

"I have no idea," I said. "I thought you'd know?"

Canzano shook his head, the gun still raised.

I glanced at Alex, then shifted my gaze back to Canzano. "Wait," I said. "So, you were there, right? You stole the appliances from Save-More Storage? But not the money?"

Canzano said, "I took back what was mine."

I didn't know what to make of what he was telling me. It was hard for me to believe there was truth to anything coming from his mouth. "What about Kathy Arnold? What do you know about her?" I looked around the property, most of it in darkness.

"How should I know?"

I didn't believe him.

I said, "Did you kill them?"

"Who?"

"Brock and Jillian?"

Canzano said, "I didn't kill nobody." He shifted his stance, the gun was still pointed at me. "So you know where my money is?"

He clearly wasn't concerned with anything else.

"*Your* money?" I said.

Canzano ran his hand through what was left of his thinning white head of hair. "I don't understand. You saw the money, but now you're telling me you don't know where it is?"

"It was there when I left," I said, without mentioning it was Kathy who took me there in the first place. I assumed he knew that already, but it was hard to know for sure.

"The money... It was in the same unit with the appliances? And the TVs?" Canzano nodded at Mike. "You look inside any of them?"

"Inside what?" Mike said.

"The washers. Dryers." Canzano turned to me. "Is that where it was? Inside one of the—"

"It was in a different unit. On the second floor."

Canzano closed his eyes and sighed, shaking his head. "Shit. I knew it." He looked at the security guard. "Why didn't you think of that?"

Mike just shrugged. "How was I supposed to know they'd put it in a different unit?"

"Who is *they*?" I said.

Canzano looked at me, like he was confused with my question. "Your buddy, Mason. And Jillian. They're the ones who ripped me off in the first place."

It wasn't exactly news to me. I'd just wished I'd gone to see Canzano sooner. "They ripped you off, but you expect me to believe you didn't kill them?"

"I'm not the only ones they ripped off. But you can believe what you want. I didn't kill them. And it's not that I didn't want to. Someone else just happened to get to them first."

Alex said, "So you know who killed them?"

Canzano shook his head. "All I'm telling you is those two stole from me. They had it coming. Jillian... I'm the one who set her up. Paid her well. But she hooked up with Mason for some reason and stabbed me in the back. I trusted both of them."

"What exactly did they do," I said. "Stole appliances from you?"

"And took my cash," he said.

"*Your* cash?" I said. "Don't you mean, money you *stole*?"

"I didn't steal money. Not technically."

"No?" I said.

"I supply the payment method. Credit cards. That's how the goods are purchased. " He had a sly smile on his face. "You'd be surprised what people throw away."

I said, "So you steal people's credit cards? From their trash?"

"Not exactly," he said, but didn't offer more.

As much as I appreciated the fact this man was openly telling me his role in crime, I was somewhat concerned why he would.

"So, you use stolen credit cards to buy appliances?" I said.

"I play a small role," he said. "Of course, you gotta have someone honest-looking to buy the goods. Jillian Rogers was just the person. She'd go in the store with the stolen credit card, make the purchase, and someone else would take it from there, turn it into cash."

"So it wasn't just you and Jillian?"

"No."

"I'm guessing you're not going to tell me who else is involved?"

"No," he said, as if he felt he'd told me enough.

"You won't tell me?"

"I don't know. There's a guy, runs the operation, but I never met him or anyone else."

"Him?" Alex said.

Canzano shrugged. "Him. Her. Could be a broad, I guess. I told you, I don't know who runs the show. All I know is too many people get involved, it always falls apart at some point."

Alex gave me a look, and I could see she was ready to get out of there.

Canzano looked at his watch, pressing a button on the side. The face of it glowed in front of him. "Hey Mikey, take care of these two, will ya? I gotta get going."

I glanced at Mike, his gun raised and now pointed at my head.

"Wait!" I said. "What do you mean by that? What's going on?"

Canzano had already started to walk away, but stopped and turned back to us. "You think I was going to tell you everything I just did, and let you walk out of here alive?" He laughed, turned, and started toward the main building.

"Wait!" I said. "What if I can help you find the money?"

Canzano stopped in his tracks, turned and looked my way and was still, like he was thinking about it. "I don't think you can," he said.

Alex lifted her shirt, came out with the Glock she had tucked in the front of her pants, and pointed it at the security guard who still had *his* gun pointed at me. "Put it down," she said, her voice calm.

"Uh, Raymond?" the guard said.

Canzano stopped and turned around, eyes wide when he saw Alex with the gun pointed at Mike. That's when he pulled his gun from his pants like he was going to fire, but Alex fired first. Then fired again, Canzano taking a step back then collapsing onto the asphalt.

The security guard was about to fire a shot, but I ducked and charged him, holding his arm up and driving him straight into the truck's rear deck. The gun went off just as it flew out of his hand.

Alex had her gun in his face when he fell to the ground.

But he didn't move.

Alex checked his pulse. "He's alive," she said, and we both looked around the area where he fell. "Did he hit his head?"

"I don't know," I said, then went over to check on Canzano.

"Is he dead?" Alex said, walking up behind me.

But Canzano's eyes were open. "You son of a bitch," he said, his voice strained and quiet. "I'll find you."

Alex was already dialing 9-1-1, and we waited until we saw the red and blue lights in the distance before we ran back to the Beemer and took off out of there before the cops showed up.

Chapter 27

"Maybe we shouldn't have left," I said, glancing over at Alex in the passenger seat. "He's going to be looking for our heads on a platter."

"You're assuming he survives," I said.

"He's not going to die. I didn't shoot to kill."

"Maybe you should have," I said.

I had the pedal to the floor, the speedometer close to eighty-five on the highway.

"Shouldn't you slow down?" Alex said.

I looked in the rearview, and noticed a set of headlights I felt had been following us for a good part of our ride since we left Canzano's.

Alex followed my eyes in the mirror and turned around to look. "What is it?" she said, then straightened out in the seat.

"I don't know. Maybe nothing. Unless someone else was at Canzano's place." I shifted my eyes from the dark road ahead to the mirror, keeping an eye on the headlights that followed us. The car seemed to be back enough of a distance I wondered if I was wrong.

"We're turning ahead," Alex said, her phone with GPS on it in her hand, the glow from it lighting up her face.

I took the next exit for Turnpike North, toward Fort Lauderdale.

Alex looked out the passenger window for a couple of moments before turning to me. "If Canzano didn't kill Brock or Jillian, then..." She paused, as if she wasn't sure what she wanted to say. "Do you ever wonder if Kathy could've done it?"

"She was with me when Brock was killed," I said.

"Well, she was likely in the hospital when it happened, if you want to get technical," Alex said. "But, I don't even mean... What I'm saying is, what if she knows who killed him? Or was behind it in some way? Don't you think that's possible?"

I kept my eyes on the road but didn't respond. "She wouldn't have called me in the first place," I said. "Why would she have me come down here, if she was going to kill her only brother?"

Alex waited before she answered. "I'm just throwing it out there. The whole thing just seems suspicious from the start."

"What I'm saying is why would she include me in on any of it?" I said, "If she had something to hide from me?"

"What if she wanted to draw attention from herself? Maybe she wanted to get you over there knowing the cops were watching?"

I cracked a smile. "I feel like you're reaching. Besides, how would she know the cops were watching? They saw both of us there."

"Yeah, but she disappeared," Alex said. "Leaving you to defend yourself. And you even said she wanted to take the money. You think she'd just change her mind, because you told her not to?"

"She was as surprised as anyone when we opened those doors. And keep in mind, she married a man with money. I don't see why she'd want to get involved in any of this, whatever Brock and Jillian were up to."

"I just don't think she's as innocent as you'd like to think," Alex said.

"I never said she was innocent at all. But she didn't kill Brock, and that's where you started with all this."

We were both quiet for a good minute or so.

I looked in the rearview and this time didn't see the same car.

Alex turned to get a look herself. "Did they turn off somewhere?"

I waited before I answered, making sure I wasn't missing something. I eased my foot off the gas and slowed down, then jumped onto the Ronald Reagan Turnpike.

I said, "Whoever followed us from the motel where Brock was hiding wasn't after me. At least I don't think they were."

"Don't be so sure," she said. "That's what I'm saying. You don't know if Kathy pulled you into this for some other reason. How do you know she's not using you, like I said, to draw the attention away from her? What if these people who've come after you think you know where that money is?"

"We're assuming that's what they're after," I said.

"Isn't that what everybody's after?" Alex said.

I laughed, shaking my head. "Not me!"

Alex didn't even crack a smile. "You shouldn't try to defend her."

"Kathy?" I said. "I'm not trying to defend her," I said. "But I can't see what reason she'd have for killing Brock."

We were both quiet again, both of us not only trying to get our heads wrapped around all that had happened, but both completely sleep deprived.

I said, "So, back to Canzano... Don't you find it strange he told us everything?"

"He told us what we wanted to hear," she said. "Are we supposed to believe he didn't kill Brock and Jillian? When he was about to kill both of us, right there on the spot?"

I nodded, like I agreed. "Then maybe we should go to the cops," I said. "Tell them everything?"

"Were you surprised he turned the camera off?" she said.

"Surprised? In what way?"

She waited a moment before she answered. "I was worried right then, why he'd do that."

"Because he turned off the camera?" I said.

"He knew he was going to take us out of the picture," she said. "Before he even started flapping his gums."

I kept my eyes on the dark road ahead, turning onto Northwest Twentieth Street. We were in Kathy and Luke's neighborhood now, most of it excessively lit with all the artificial light you could ever ask for, from the streetlamps and porch lights.

I heard a siren in the distance, growing louder by the second, that was soon followed by blue lights filling up the neighborhood. Two police vehicles took the corner, coming toward us.

"Oh no," Alex said, with worry apparent in her voice.

"They can't be for us," I said. "There's no way Canzano would tell the cops the truth about what happened back there."

"You're right," Alex said, turning in the seat to look out the back.

I pulled over to the side of the street when the blue lights got closer, flooding the inside of the BMW when the police vehicle blew past us at full speed.

Another police vehicle came from the opposite direction ahead of us and turned hard down Kathy and Luke's street, almost on two wheels when it took the turn.

I pulled out and drove ahead, turning down the same street after the two police vehicles.

I stopped one house away from Luke and Kathy's house, both of us waiting, watching the cops run from their cars and across the lawn.

"What do we do?" I said, the car still in drive, my foot down on the brake.

The blue lights were all flashing, the vehicles empty.

I heard more sirens in the distance, this time followed by red lights turning the corner.

An EMT vehicle went past us and drove across the lawn, then backed up around the side of the house.

More sirens could be heard in the distance, growing louder.

I stepped out of the car.

"What are you doing?" Alex said. "You sure we should go back there?"

I didn't answer, hurrying across the lawn and toward the back of the house.

The EMT vehicle had backed all the way onto the lawn in the backyard and parked by a ground-level wooden deck. A spotlight on the vehicle lit up all of the grass and four cops standing back there, almost in a circle.

I got closer and saw two paramedics crouched down over a body in the grass.

I took a few steps closer without anybody noticing, until I was just a few feet from whoever was on the ground.

Luke Arnold lay in his boxer shorts and nothing else, blood covering the area around his chest.

"Is he alive?" I said, and the four officers turned to me. "Who are you?" one of them said. I recognized the taller one from my hotel.

"Henry Walsh," I said.

Nobody had answered me at first. I don't think anyone knew for sure. But then the paramedic stood and said to the cops, "We're too late."

Luke Arnold was dead.

Chapter 28

IT WAS BARELY SIX in the morning and I'd left Alex asleep, going outside to get some much-needed air after nonstop rolling for the handful of hours since we'd gotten back to the hotel.

The police had no indication of who could have killed Luke Arnold, and I couldn't help but wonder if Kathy had ended up, instead, with the same fate as her husband.

The air outside the hotel was somewhat cool but still humid. The sun was starting to rise, a tint of orange bleeding into the sky above it.

Neither Detective Collins nor Detective Helms had returned my calls. Of course, it was in the middle of the night when I called. But I was surprised neither had arrived at the scene behind Luke Arnold's house while Alex and I were still there.

I was afraid of the finger-pointing that could come my way, considering there was obvious friction between me and Kathy's husband, most of it directed toward me, from him, than the other way around.

I knew how these things often went, and how quickly cops liked to jump on a suspect.

I'd taken my phone from my pocket to look at the screen, when I glanced up and saw a Miami-Dade police vehicle turn into the parking lot, practically jumping the curb, blue lights flashing but no siren.

The car stopped in the circular drive in front of me. A single uniformed officer jumped out and rushed toward the entrance. Even though it was still somewhat dark outside, the cop wore dark sunglasses and a Miami-Dade PD baseball cap pulled down tight to where the hat's bill met his sunglasses.

I was about to step out of his way, but he pulled a gun and held it on me, the gun gripped with both hands. "Hands against the wall!"

I looked behind me, as if there was a chance he was talking to someone else. But there was nobody else around. Even the lobby was empty. I didn't do as I was asked.

So the cop grabbed my arms and spun me around, throwing me up against the wall. My face smashed into the Stucco exterior.

"What the hell did I do?" I said.

All I could think was it had something to do with Luke Arnold's death.

But the cop didn't say a word, throwing the cuffs on my wrists, then taking my wallet from my pocket.

I glanced over my shoulder and saw him look at one of my business cards, then tossed the wallet on the ground.

"What the hell are you—"

The cop punched me in the back of the head. "Shut your mouth!" He then pushed me toward his car and into the back seat.

"You didn't even read me my rights," I said, the rear door slamming in my face.

The cop was not a small man by any means, wedging himself into the front seat behind the wheel.

I still hadn't gotten a good enough look at him, until I looked into the rearview. He still had the sunglasses on, but it hit me who he was. "It's you!" I said. "From the park!"

I felt my phone buzzing in my pocket, but with my hands cuffed behind my back, there was nothing I could do to answer it. But when I looked out of the car and into the hotel lobby, I could see Alex running on the other side of the glass toward the hotel's entrance, the phone to her ear.

The cop took off, and all I could do was look out at Alex, chasing after us barefoot and in a T-shirt and shorts, the way she was in bed before I left.

The cop hit the same curb leaving the parking lot as he had coming in, and I bounced in the seat and slid almost to the other side when he cut the wheel hard, driving into oncoming traffic. He picked up the phone and said, "Got him. Be there in ten."

I didn't recognize the area we were driving through. But I at least knew the turn for the Miami-Dade Police headquarters.

When we drove past it, I knew I was in bigger trouble than if he *had* taken me to the police station.

I looked out the back window after the so-called cop missed the turn. I watched the guy looking straight ahead toward the road. "You're not a cop, are you," I said.

He didn't seem to react in any way whatsoever, driving straight, doing the speed limit as if not in much of a hurry, until we passed the sign for Miami Lakes.

Things were about to go from bad to worse.

He turned into the parking lot of what looked to be an abandoned church, continuing straight and around to the back where two cars were parked.

He left the engine running and got out of the vehicle, came around to my side and opened the door. "Let's go."

"Go where?" I said, not willing or ready to so easily follow his command.

He reached in and pulled me out of the car, yanking at my arm and dragging me across a walkway. With my hands behind my back, there was little I could do about it. Leading me to a door at the back of the church, he knocked.

The door opened into darkness, and he pushed me inside, slamming the door behind me. The man apparently stayed outside, and left me alone—from what I could tell—in total darkness.

I heard the engine roar from the other side of the door outside, then slowly fade away.

"Hello?" I said, waiting for my eyes to adjust.

When they finally did, I could make out two figures in front of me. But it was too dark to see their faces.

"Who are you?" I said. "What do you want?"

A flashlight came on, shining in my face. The man holding the light on me wore a ski mask.

I lost track of the other figure, but was startled when I felt hands on my arms from behind me. I was thrown to the floor, turning my shoulder enough to break my fall.

I was dragged along the floor by the handcuffs on my wrists, the metal digging into my skin. "Christ," I said. "I can walk, you know."

The flashlight went off and I was lifted from the ground and thrown onto a chair that nearly tipped over as I landed on it.

"Tell us where the money is," one of the two men said, his voice deep and not one I recognized.

I should've known.

"What money?" I said.

One of the men punched me in the face, and I felt the warmth of my own blood drip from my mouth. "Don't play stupid," the man said. "You have two minutes to tell us where you put that money."

"Are you deaf?" I said. "I didn't take any money."

What I did take was another hit to the face, this time with what felt like the back of a very large hand.

The flashlight was again shined in my face and I squeezed my eyes closed, turning my head with blood dripping down my chin.

One of the men got behind me again, this time grabbing a clump of my hair and pulling my head back. I opened my eyes enough to see he had a knife in his hand, coming toward my throat where he rested the blade just under my Adam's apple.

"This is your last chance," the man said, standing behind me. I could feel the sharpness of the blade "You have ten seconds."

Ten seconds wasn't a lot of time to talk my way out of most situations, certainly not one where I had a knife against my throat.

I had my hands into a position where I could grip the back of what felt like a metal folding chair. I wouldn't have much leverage, and the chance of what I was cooking up in my head backfiring was strong.

But I didn't have a choice. I didn't have whatever these two clowns were asking for, and didn't think it would be smart for me to wait and see if I could call their bluff.

"Seven seconds," the man behind me said, the knife still up to my throat.

Without a lot of thinking, I gripped the back of the chair and jumped to my feet, feeling the knife's blade cut into my skin. But I threw as much of my weight as I could backward. I came to my feet and spun my body around with the chair in my grasp behind me, first knocking the knife to the floor, by the sound of it, then coming around again, letting the chair fly. I heard a yelp, with the sound of a heavy thud. I turned and saw the man behind me on the floor, then charged the one holding the flashlight in front of me, driving him straight back with as much force as I could bring, only stopping when we crashed into the wall on the other side of the room.

We both fell to the floor and I stumbled as I got up to my feet.

A gunshot rang out with a flash lighting up the dark room.

I wasn't sure where the shot had come from, but didn't feel any additional pain, other than the cut on my neck and from the punches I'd taken to the face.

I heard a grunt from the man underneath me. "You shot me, you son of a bitch."

I knew he couldn't have been talking to me.

The flashlight was on the floor, the light shining toward a door I ran for and crashed through, falling to the ground when I got to the other side. I struggled to get to my feet without much use of my hands, but stood up in the middle of what I believed was called the sanctuary, although the pews had all been removed. There was a cross on the back wall, but it was crooked and looked to be ready to fall.

Another shot was fired at me when one of the men came through the same doorway I'd crashed through. He had his gun pointed at me, fired another shot, and took out the glass from a window no more than three or four feet over my head.

I ran, hands cuffed behind my back, and crashed through a door, landing on the concrete walkway outside. But I didn't think I could outrun this man, so I stopped just outside the door and waited.

He came running outside after me, and I smashed into him as hard as I could, knocking him to the ground. His gun fired into the air as I kicked it from his hand, then dropped on top of him with both knees.

Something inside him cracked, and he let out a childlike scream.

I struggled to get back to my feet, running as fast as I could. I didn't stop until I'd made it out into traffic onto Ludlam Road, and continued running as fast as I could. Traffic was heavy going both ways, horns blowing at me trying to get across to the other side.

I kept going, breathing heavy, my mouth dry. I made it to an intersection, the signs reading Northwest Sixty-Seventh and Ludlam. That's where I spotted a Miami Lakes police vehicle stopped at the light.

Of course, the officer behind the wheel saw me—a man running in traffic and in handcuffs—and jumped from his car, leaving the driver-side door open.

I slowed down and waited when I saw him coming after me, explaining as much as I could, hoping he'd believe me, before he reacted in a way I'd regret.

Chapter 29

I sat in a chair next to a metal desk at the Miami Lakes Police headquarters. It was fairly quiet there, six or so officers hanging around or sitting at desks, some on the phone, others chatting with each other like they were having a good time. The officer who picked me up from the intersection, Officer Cardwell, was on the phone with someone over at the Miami-Dade PD after I'd told him just about everything I could.

I caught most of the conversation, but he cleared a few things up for me as soon as he hung up the phone.

"A police car was stolen from a 7-Eleven this afternoon," he said, rubbing his hand over the dark stubble growing on his face.

"So the chances are good he wasn't a cop," I said.

"They actually had officers out there looking for you. Apparently someone you know showed up at the station asking for details about why you were arrested. But nobody, for obvious reasons, knew what she was talking about."

Alex.

I said, "Can I make a call?"

The cop nodded and got up. "Go ahead," he said, then got up and walked away. I dialed Alex.

"Henry?" she said, answering on the first ring. I could hear the nerves in her voice. "Where are you?"

"I'm at the police station. Miami Lakes."

"Miami Lakes?" she said. "Are you okay?"

"Yeah, I'm fine. It wasn't a real cop."

"I know," she said. "Can I come get you?"

"I wish you would," I said.

"I'll be there soon." Alex hung up and I held on to my phone, looking around at the other cops.

Officer Cardwell came back over with a white foam cup, placing it on the desk. "You want a coffee?"

"No, thank you." I said, "Is anyone at that church yet? Kathy has to be in there somewhere." I sighed. "I should have looked for her."

"From what it sounds like, you would have been dead if you didn't get out of there," he said, placing a hand on my shoulder. "It'll be all right. We'll find her."

I think he was underestimating the situation, but I was glad Cardwell seemed to be a nice, levelheaded cop.

He sat back down behind his desk. "There's a detective over there at Miami-Dade, wanted to come by to talk to you," he said. "I don't know her, personally."

"Detective Collins?" I said.

"Yeah, that's her," Cardwell said. "She wanted to come over to talk to you, but I told her we had no reason to hold you, and couldn't promise you'd be here when she showed up."

"She say anything else?" I said.

Officer Cardwell shook his head. "She was somewhat short with me." He picked up his cell phone and keys from the desk.

"I'm going to head over to the church, see what else they've found. If you want to take a ride out..."

"I've got someone coming for me," I said.

Cardwell leaned against the desk, arms folded. "You know, I don't know if you're familiar with that church at all, but it's been closed for at least a couple years. They built one of those mega churches, looks like some kind of corporate office building now, half a mile from there. I'm not sure who owns the old church now. Last I heard, they were hoping to build apartments on the land. Not sure we need more apartments around, but..." He leaned back in his chair.

"I'm just glad you believed me," I said. "I know it's supposed to be innocent until proven guilty, but I've met enough cops in my day who like to turn that one around."

Cardwell grinned. "Well, other than the fact you're running down the street with your hands cuffed behind your back... If you'd been arrested by a real cop, we would've known about it. Gotta have balls, drive around like that in a stolen police vehicle."

I thought for a moment. "The thing is, I wonder how he'd get his hands on a uniform like he wore. It wasn't just some store-bought Halloween costume, either. It was all legit... I'd say it was an official Miami-Dade uniform. Can't imagine you just buy those off the street around here."

Officer Cardwell pulled at his chin, shaking his head. "I don't believe he's a real cop, if that's what you're—"

"I'm saying he could've been. Formerly, I mean. Or knows someone on the inside."

"Well, we're going to find him," he said. He looked at his watch. "You said you've got a ride?"

"She should be here soon," I said. "You don't have to wait around, if you want to get over there."

Cardwell shook his head, picking up the Styrofoam cup. "I'll wait," he said. "Your friend who was killed, you said you came down to help him, before he was killed?"

"It's been a mess," I said.

"I dug up what I could, but there are quite a few holes in the case, from what I could find."

"Are you familiar with any of it?" I said.

Cardwell shook his head. "I saw the reports about your friend who's been missing, but we don't get involved in much of what's going on with Miami-Dade PD. Not unless it happens right here in Miami Lakes."

I said, "I thought I was coming down to Miami to get to the truth, see if I could clear his name. Turned out it was nothing but lies from the start. He and his girlfriend were allegedly involved in some kind of theft ring, stealing appliances... TVs... Someone would flip them for cash."

"And these are friends of yours?" Cardwell said, his nose crinkled.

"Well, I knew Brock a long time ago. And his sister, but..."

"So who killed who?" he said.

"Well, that's the question," I said.

Officer Cardwell went back to his chair and sat behind the desk. He opened his laptop and started to type. "What are the other names? The victims?"

"You mean, besides Brock and Jillian? Her ex-husband, Steve Rogers was killed the night he wanted to meet me."

Cardwell looked up from the laptop. "Steve Rogers?" He typed on the keyboard.

"Then, last night Luke Arnold was killed."

"That's your friend's husband, right? The woman who's missing?"

"Yes, sir," I said.

Cardwell looked at the screen in front of him. "Says here Luke Arnold... Looks like somebody may've tried to break into his home."

"That may or may not be the case," I said.

Cardwell leaned back in his chair. "So, how do you know your buddy, Mason... how do you know for sure he didn't kill the girlfriend?"

"I don't," I said. "Nobody knows much of anything about what might've happened to her. He claims he was set up, someone making it look like he did it. Even got a call she was up in Jacksonville, which turned out not to be true. Don't take this personally," I said, "but I'm surprised your department hasn't had any involvement in any of this."

Cardwell didn't seem to be offended, shaking his head with a slight shrug. "We're a small community here in Miami Lakes. Small department. Murder, kidnapping... you're usually going to see Miami-Dade controlling the ball, even if it's here in Miami Lakes. But, I guess you'd say I'm kind of surprised myself; it's almost like the communications outside Miami-Dade PD had been shut down."

A door opened a few feet from Cardwell's desk, and an older woman poked her head out. She said, "Rob, a Ms. Jepson is out here for, uh"—she looked down at a pad she had in her hand— "Henry Walsh?"

"Yeah, this is him right here," Cardwell said, pointing at me with his thumb.

We both stood from the desk and I followed him down a short hall, into the main lobby.

Alex was standing with her back to us, looking out the glass front toward the street, but turned when I said her name.

She rushed over to me and gave me a quick hug, easing up as if she didn't want to overdo any kind of public display of affection.

We were both in agreement on that topic.

"This is Officer Cardwell," I said, introducing the two. "This is Alex."

He reached out and shook her hand. "Rob," he said, then turned to me. "I'm heading over to the church, see if they've come up with anything." He had his phone in his hand, and gave the screen a quick glance when it vibrated. "Oh, let me get this." He turned from us to answer. I heard him say, "Got something?" then glanced back at me over his shoulder, listening to the caller. "All right, thanks." He put his phone on his belt. "No sign of anyone else up there," he said. "But we'll continue looking. Miami-Dade was supposed to send one of their detectives over there, but apparently nobody's shown up."

"Kind of odd, isn't it?" I said.

Cardwell gave me a business card. "You need anything from me, don't hesitate to reach out."

Alex and I went outside and walked to the Camry she'd rented, parked a half block away.

I stood outside the passenger side. "You know what I was thinking when I was in the back of that police cruiser?"

Alex stopped before she got in, looking at me across the roof.

"Retirement," I said. "I don't know if I can do this anymore. And I mean for good this time. Maybe 'retirement' isn't the right word. Maybe it's just called quitting."

She didn't respond, or say a word back to me. She knew I'd said it before. I *had* quit. I'd tried to walk away. But something—someone—always sucked me back in.

"We have to find Kathy," she said. "Then, we can worry about the future."

"Worry?" I said. "That's what I don't want to do anymore. I'm sick of always being worried."

She held her gaze on me for a moment, then cracked a slight smile before she finally got in and behind the wheel.

I got in the passenger side and Alex was waiting, watching me. She had a look on her face I couldn't read, like she wanted to smile, but couldn't. Or maybe it was a look of concern, wondering how foolish it would be to marry a man who never really had his head on straight.

......

We stopped in front of the church but there didn't seem to be much action other than two Miami Lakes police vehicles. There was no sign of anyone from the Miami-Dade Police Department. I'd already left Detective Collins a message to call me, but had yet to hear back.

Alex had her phone out now, her thumbs moving at a rapid pace over the screen. She turned it to me, with a photo of the church we were sitting in front of, the headline of the article reading, "Local Developer Purchases Church, City Approves Zoning Change."

I said, "Does it say who owns it?"

Alex took the phone back, looking at the screen. "His name's Jason Peters."

"Maybe we should track him down," I said.

Alex said, "Just because he owns it doesn't mean he allowed someone to use it to abduct a private investigator from Fernandina Beach."

She was right. There was a chance whoever owned it had no connection whatsoever to the men who had grabbed me.

It had started to rain, the skies as dark as I'd seen them since I got to Miami. The drops sounded like pebbles hitting the metal roof.

"I would guess the cops are going to talk to Mr. Peters," I said. "But it doesn't mean we shouldn't."

Alex had her eyes on the screen when they opened wide and she again turned the phone to me. "This man, Jason Peters—the one who owns the church property..." She paused. "He used to own a place called Magic City TV and Appliance. It was a local chain, with six locations. Filed bankruptcy four months ago."

We both looked at each other.

She said, "Allegedly, a string of thefts wiped them out."

I couldn't believe it.

Alex studied her phone. "It says here the stores had been in his family for over fifty years. But business had been getting worse since the son, Jason Peters, took over."

I thought about it. "So, maybe this guy's business is collapsing. He partners up with someone who goes in and makes purchases, most likely with stolen credit cards. Completely wipes out their inventory, maybe he even collects insurance of some sort... But the business is done."

Alex said, "A lot of assumptions here. But... Let's say he's involved. Gets a cut of whoever buys this stuff off the black market, so he can hide it from the creditors he'll owe."

"It doesn't sound that far-fetched," I said. "But how does the guy go bankrupt, then ends up investing in real estate? Leave it to the rich, get to screw up a dozen times over and somehow still end up ahead of the rest of us."

Alex was on her phone again, and I could see in her eyes there was something else she'd dug up. She turned the phone to me. "Look."

I took the phone from her and gazed at a picture of three high school kids in basketball uniforms, arms around each other. The phone was from the digital archives of the *Miami Post*. "What is this?"

"Read the caption," she said, taking the phone back from me. "It says, Jason Peters, Gary Helms, and Steve Rogers celebrate their championship game against South Miami High School."

Chapter 30

I WAS ALMOST SURPRISED to hear Detective Collins was at the station, after I'd called her a handful of times on the ride over, leaving her three different messages. But even though I was told she was there, I ended up waiting for her in the lobby for close to thirty minutes.

Detective Collins finally showed her face, coming through the door with a large envelope tucked under her arm. "I don't have a lot of time," she said, walking toward me, looking at her phone.

"I've been calling you," I said. "I know you spoke with Officer Cardwell up in Miami Lakes, but—"

"Will you please tell me why you're here," she said, as if I was just some stranger coming in off the street.

She didn't ask me if I was okay, or for any details about what had happened. Nothing about the so-called cop in the stolen police vehicle, either. It didn't add up.

"I think I've found something," I said, my voice hushed. The officer behind the desk was watching us. "It's important."

She didn't seem to want to make eye contact with me, or I thought maybe it was that her mind was somewhere else.

"Can we talk somewhere?" I said. "In private?"

She seemed to roll her eyes and let out a sigh, then finally nodded as she turned for the door she'd just come out from. "I told you already, I don't have much time."

"You'll want to hear this," I said, and followed her through the door.

Collins stayed a few steps ahead of me without looking back, then turned down a busy hall with officers in conversation standing in front of us along the way.

"Excuse us," Collins said, and continued down another hall that was empty, as if an area somewhat off the beaten path, a handful of empty offices with lights turned off on either side of the hall.

She led me into a windowless conference room with a small table in the corner and stacks of cardboard file boxes against the wall. She turned to me once we entered the room and waited for me to enter, then closed the door behind me.

"What is it that's so important," she said, more of a statement than a question, as if telling me to hurry up and get on with it. Her arms were folded, the envelope still in her hand.

I looked around, wondering if I should sit, but she clearly wasn't interested in any kind of extended chat.

I said, "I wouldn't say this is actual evidence, but I do feel I have a lead for you." I paused, trying to get a read of her expressionless face. "The thing is, you're probably not going to like what I'm going to show you."

"What kind of a lead?" she said, finally giving me her attention.

I wasn't exactly sure how to approach it, wondering how she'd react. It could go one of many ways. "Can I ask you... How long have you known Detective Helms?"

"How long have I known him?"

I waited for her to answer, the young detective staring back at me, opening her mouth to speak, closing it then clearing her throat.

"Exactly what is it you're asking me?" she said. "Because I don't understand what you—"

"How well do you know him?" I said.

She seemed to have trouble with her answer. "I... I've known Detective Helms for... I don't know. A few years? If you have something to say," she said, "I wish you'd get to the point. I told you, I don't have a lot of time." She looked at her watch, then opened the door and nervously peered outside, as if to make sure we were alone before closing it again.

I said, "Did you know he went to high school with Jillian Rogers' ex-husband?"

Collins held her gaze, as if frozen, before shifting her stance and walking across the room to the single window overlooking the parking lot. "What does this have to do with anything?"

"Think about it," I said. "Did you know he knew Steve Rogers?"

She turned to me with a look like she was thinking it through. "Are you trying to imply that because a police detective went to high school with someone he may or may have not have even known... Are you trying to say you believe Detective Helms is somehow connected to—"

"I told you it's not real evidence. But if he never told you, or anyone else, that he knew Steve Rogers?"

She huffed out a nervous laugh. "Whatever it is you're trying to imply... this is the most ridiculous thing I've ever heard." She opened the door. "Stop wasting my time with your nonsense, Mr. Walsh."

"Wait," I said. "Didn't you talk to Steve Rogers after Jillian's death?" I said. "He stayed close with her, even after their divorce. And then, he calls me to meet him and ends up dead? Come to find out, Detective Helms knew the man personally? Don't you find it odd, Helms or even Steve Rogers never mentioned it to you?"

"I think you should have stopped when you stated you didn't have any evidence," Collins said. "You can't just come in here, try making accusations about a fellow officer, just because you dug up some old photo online."

I thought back through our brief conversation.

I was sure I hadn't said a word about the photo.

I had to figure out my next move. Was she covering for him? Did she know more than she'd let on?

"Maybe I've got it all wrong," I said. "Sorry to waste your time."

She held her gaze, eyes right on mine, like she was trying to see through them.

"Maybe as a private investigator you can trust your gut, try to point fingers without any evidence. But that's not how we do things around here. I'm sorry." She gestured for me to go out the door ahead of her, then grabbed my arm. "I think it would be best if you kept this quiet. For your own sake."

I nodded, trying to hide my swallow. I took it as a threat, but didn't ask for any kind of clarification.

She walked out ahead of me. " I'll talk to Detective Helms, just to make sure there's nothing he's not telling me. I doubt there is, but..."

"I hope you don't allow your relationship to get in the way of the truth," I said.

She stopped and turned to me, her finger in my face. "I told you once, and I'm not going to tell you again; don't tell me how to do my job, Mr. Walsh." She started to walk ahead, but stopped short once again. "Don't you think maybe it's time for you and your friend to go home to Jacksonville?"

"I don't live in Jacksonville," I said, as if that small piece of misinformation mattered. I couldn't help making the correction. I said, "But either way, if you think I'm actually going to leave Miami at this point..."

Collins continued ahead of me down the hall at a fast pace, clearly in a hurry and done listening to me. She stopped at the door to the lobby, opened it, and waited for me to walk through, then grabbed me by the arm. She got close to me, whispering into my ear. "I'm warning you, Walsh. Stay out of this."

Before I even made it over the threshold, Collins slammed the door closed behind me, the door smacking me in the back.

Chapter 31

Alex and I sat in the hotel, unsure of where to go next. Alex had her laptop out, tapping away on the keys, digging deeper into the internet, beyond the virtual walls most of us never penetrate within the dark web. She was good at finding information even the cops couldn't dig up on someone's background or past. But this time, she wasn't having much luck making any kind of present connection between Detective Helms and either of the two men in that high school photo.

I watched Alex and noticed the look on her face like she'd found something, leaning closer to the laptop's screen. She raised her gaze. "Did you know Detective Collins was married?"

"Was?" I said.

"Her husband died eleven months ago."

"Oh," I said. "I didn't know."

"Cancer," she said, eyes on the computer.

I sat, quietly waiting for more, a lump in my throat. If anyone knew what it was like to lose her husband at a young age, it was Alex.

I got up from the chair and leaned on the back of hers, looking down at her laptop in front of her. "You found this on the dark web?"

Alex glanced up at me. "It's an archive of old websites and pages. The one I found is a page from a peer-to-peer fundraising site, where you ask people—friends or family, usually—to help pay for things like medical expenses."

She was quiet, reading what was in front of her.

"You think there's a chance she was trying to raise money for her husband?" I said.

Alex didn't answer right away, studying the text in front of her. "It looks like she closed the account before raising anything at all. The money would be for a drug trial she'd hoped could've saved her husband."

"It says all that right there?" I said.

Alex nodded. "It looks like she wrote it all out, but never ended up going through with it."

"With the drug trial? Or the fundraising?"

Alex wiped her cheek with her hand.

I said, "So, tell me again how you found this?"

"I was just looking for anything, see what I could find out about her. There's certainly something suspicious about how she acted with you earlier. But, this..."

"I guess it's true," I said, "whatever you do online never truly disappears, no matter what you try to do."

"That's a fact," Alex said. "Even something like this, she likely didn't want it out there, seeing she clearly must've changed her mind."

"Or maybe it was because he died," I said.

Alex shook her head. "No, it was four months earlier."

Alex typed on the laptop, reading on the screen. Her eyes opened wide. "Wow," she said. "Some of these trials run close to a hundred grand."

"Are you serious?" I said. "For a drug nobody knows'll work?"

"I guess it depends," she said, then started frantically typing on the laptop.

I thought about it. "That's the pharmaceutical industry for you. Gotta be able to pay for those Hollywood-style commercials they run every five minutes. Of course, you can go to Canada, get the same drug for five bucks."

Alex didn't respond, focused instead on digging deeper, fingers moving furiously on the keyboard. She stopped. "I can't find anything."

"What else?" I said.

"What treatment trial he might've been involved in, if at all."

"You mean if they didn't have the money?"

Alex shrugged.

I said, "There was some kind of drug that came out for Alzheimer's, but it was over fifty grand. I guess it's only for rich people." I walked to the window and looked outside. "Only in America."

Alex closed her laptop. "So, where do we go from here?"

"Wait," I said. "You didn't find anything else about it?"

Alex and I were both quiet for a couple of moments.

I said, "I feel bad for her. But it doesn't excuse her from not acting on what I told her."

"You don't think she'll approach him about it?"

"It didn't appear that way," I said. "She was far from convinced by anything I told her. But maybe she was right. Maybe that photo…" It hit me. "I didn't tell you. She mentioned the photo to me. But I hadn't mentioned it."

"What do you mean you didn't mention it?"

I thought about how tired I was. I couldn't remember the last time I'd slept, and how my brain was clearly not working the way I needed it to.

"I can't believe I didn't tell you," I said. "All I told Detective Collins was I knew Helms went to school with the other two. But she mentioned a photo…"

Alex stood up from the chair. "Then she knows about it," she said. "And it's not just a coincidence those three men were in that photo together. All we have to do is establish their present-day connections, all these years later. But that should be easy."

"But it's not enough," I said, looking back out the window. "We have nothing substantial. We need real evidence." I looked at my watch. "I say we go talk to Helms."

Alex shook her head. "Maybe if you hadn't told Collins. At this point, she's probably either confronted him, or warned him of what we know."

"So then what would be the harm in confronting him my-self?"

Alex pulled at her chin, then gave a quick nod. "Let's go. I'll drive."

· · · • · • · · ·

I was back in the lobby at Miami-Dade headquarters, waiting for Detective Helms. The older officer at the front desk said he'd talked to him directly, and that Helms told him he'd be right out. But a good twenty minutes had already gone by. I was starting to wonder.

I went up to the cop behind the desk, smiling with his eyes on the computer in front of him like he was looking at something that had little to do with police work. "Excuse me," I said. "You sure Detective Helms knows I'm out here?"

The cop rolled his eyes, as if he didn't want to be bothered. "I'll check." He picked up the phone, the handset against his ear, waiting. He finally said into the phone, "Hey, is Detective Helms back there?" A confused look took over his face. "Oh, okay. Thanks." He hung up the phone, pointing to it with his thumb. "Apparently, Detective Helms had to step out."

"He left?" I said. "After I got here?"

The cop just shrugged. "I'm sorry, but..."

I turned and dashed out the door, rushing down the concrete steps and across the street to where Alex was waiting behind the wheel.

I jumped into the passenger seat. I said, "He took off."

"What do you mean he took off?" Alex said. She shifted into drive. "Did anyone say where he went?"

"I don't know," I said. "Maybe we can find his house."

Alex pulled out of the parking space and onto Northwest Twenty-Fifth. "I already put it in my phone. I looked it up while you were in there."

She was always a step ahead of me.

I turned in my seat, looking out the back window toward the building I'd just walked out of. "This all seems way too suspicious."

"So you didn't talk to him?" Alex said. "You were in there a while."

"He never came out. I was trying to be patient. But he must've taken off as soon as he heard my name."

"Do you think Detective Collins spoke to him?"

"I don't know. Probably," I said. "Maybe she did warn him."

"It's also possible he had police business to deal with," she said. "Before you jump the gun."

"Don't you think he would've had the courtesy to come out, tell me he couldn't talk?" I shook my head. "I don't think so. This guy knows something."

Alex stopped at a red light, typed into her phone and placed it in the holder on the dashboard with the GPS turned on. She said, "He lives in Hialeah. One forty-five West Fifty-Seventh." She turned up the volume on her phone, the digital voice telling us to take the next left.

Alex turned onto the ramp for 826, heading north, as the GPS instructed her to do.

"We should probably be careful," I said. "But if by chance he's got something to hide, he's not going to stick around."

Chapter 32

We pulled off of 826 when a blue SUV drove past us heading in the other direction on West Fifty-Seventh. I watched out the back passenger window as it drove by, seeing Detective Helms behind the wheel of his Dodge Durango, speeding past us.

"That was him!" I said.

Alex spun the Toyota around, tires screeching, and slammed her foot on the gas as she straightened out the wheel.

We raced after Helms.

"Don't let him see you," I said. "If he's the one who's been following my every move, then he'll know this car. Just stay back. Let's see where he's going."

Alex took her foot off the gas, but continued after Helms, following him for another five miles until we saw the sign for Miami International Airport.

"He can't be getting on a plane," Alex said. "Can he?" She looked over at me, as if I knew the answer.

I was afraid we were getting too close to him. "Ease back a little," I said.

Alex said, "Do you want to drive?" sounding annoyed.

With the heavy traffic around the airport, she had no choice but to slow down anyway.

Helms changed lanes, shifting into the one on the far left, where a sign read Short-Term Parking. He took the turn.

"Don't lose him," I said, knowing Alex was going to smack me if I kept doing the backseat driving.

She said, "You want me to go slow? Or speed up? Make up your mind." She gave me a look, rolling her eyes. "Relax, Henry. I've got it."

Helms stopped and reached out at the ticket machine a few cars ahead of us, then started onto the circular ramp. He was getting too far ahead of us, and continued upward without slowing down.

I was afraid we'd lost him. "Did you see which level he pulled onto?"

Alex didn't answer, speeding up the circular ramp after she pulled the ticket, continuing upward in circles until we got to the seventh level: the roof.

Alex drove ahead but slowed, both of us looking through the dozens of rows of parked cars.

"Do you see him?" I said, the window down now, my head sticking out so I could get a better view. The lot was mostly full, with few open spots as far as I could see.

Finally, Alex pointed straight toward the lane ahead of us. "Down there."

I saw the back of Helms' SUV, driving down the lane between the two last rows on the terminal side.

Alex drove in the same direction. "What do you want me to do? I can't get too close."

"Let me out," I said, opening the door before she'd stopped. I jumped out onto the hot concrete as soon as she stopped.

Moving quickly between the rows of parked cars, staying low enough I wouldn't be seen, I headed in the direction I believed Helms had gone.

I could see where he pulled into a space and parked where there were no other cars, although a van was parked four or five spaces from him. I couldn't tell if anyone was inside, and it didn't look like anyone had gotten out.

Helms stepped out of his SUV and pulled a cigarette pack from his top shirt pocket, sticking a smoke in his mouth. He looked around and leaned against the rear bumper on his Dodge. The cigarette was lit, and he straightened up from his vehicle, looking my way.

I ducked down behind a parked car, watching through a window, hoping he couldn't see me.

But then I looked out toward the driving lane between the rows of parked cars, and watched a maroon Chevrolet Impala driving slowly past me.

It was Detective Collins, heading toward the area where Helms was waiting.

Alex came up behind me, her hand on my shoulder. "What's he doing?"

"Did you see who just drove by?" I said.

Alex nodded. "The Impala?"

"It's Detective Collins."

Alex straightened up enough to get a better look, removing her sunglasses as she peered over the car's roof. "Are you sure?"

"I saw her behind the wheel," I said.

Alex and I watched, waiting as Collins pulled her car next to Helms' Dodge, but she didn't get out at first.

Helms took another drag from his cigarette, then turned and opened the hatch on his SUV.

I moved a little closer, behind another car, trying to get a better look without Helms or Collins seeing me.

Helms had the hatch open now, lifting the rug panel up in the cargo area in the back of his vehicle. He came out with a folder he held in one hand, the cigarette dangling from his lips.

Collins opened the driver-side door on her Impala and stepped out.

The conversation quickly became animated between the two, but I couldn't make out what they were saying. Not until Helms raised his voice, yelling at her: "If you hadn't killed Jillian, none of this would have happened!"

Alex looked at me and I could see the shock on her face, and assumed she saw the same look on mine.

Neither of us said a word, but Alex took out her phone and started to record what we were witnessing.

"Good thinking," I whispered.

Helms took one more drag from his cigarette, then flicked it to the ground. He appeared to be calmer now, saying something else to Collins, but stopped and looked toward a plane that had just taken off.

I felt the plane's deep and powerful roar, a whooshing, high-pitched whine, the plane climbing into the air directly over our heads. I felt the rumbling under my feet and looked up at the plane, but then shifted my gaze back to the two detectives.

Collins had a gun pointed at Helms. With the ear-piercing noise from the plane, it was hard to tell at first she'd fired a shot. Helms grabbed his chest and with his other arm reached up high, as if trying to grab the air, only to stumble back a few steps and collapse into the rear quarter of his SUV. He fell to one knee, the folder and papers on the ground around him.

Collins pointed her gun at Helms and fired once more. This time, the sound of it was more evident, though still largely masked by the sound from the plane.

Helms crumbled to the pavement.

Collins rushed to him, her hand under his jaw, then picked up the papers and hurried to her car.

Alex dialed her phone and put it to her ear, both of us staying low and out of sight.

Collins backed from her parking space and took off down the lane between the parked cars, blowing past us at full speed.

I hurried over to Helms facedown on the hot concrete, blood splattered on the back bumper of his Dodge and puddled underneath him.

I knew he was gone, but grabbed his wrist to check his pulse, just in case.

Detective Gary Helms was dead.

Alex stood behind me, on the phone with 9-1-1. "Go get her," she said, throwing me the keys. "I'll wait here."

I ran from Alex without saying another word, already hearing sirens nearby. I felt a sense of shock, still having a hard time believing what we'd just witnessed.

I jumped into the car and looked ahead toward the exit. Mia Collins was already gone. Taking off after her, I glanced in the rearview at Alex standing by the body, watching me drive away.

The Toyota hit the edge of the ramp with a hard thump, the bottom scraping the concrete. Racing after Collins, I circled each level of the lot but had to slam on the brakes when a car pulled out in front of me from the second level.

I yelled, "Get out of the way!" and laid on the horn.

The car moved at a snail's pace, the driver appearing oblivious.

When we were finally at the exit where I could pass, the woman behind the wheel threw me an unfriendly gesture, blowing her own high-pitched horn.

Luckily, Mia Collins was in my sights, but speeding under the blue sign with an arrow pointing down that read AIRPORT EXIT.

I slid a credit card into the ticket machine, and had to wait a couple of moments until the gate's arm finally went up.

Collins had slowed down to the speed limit, driving along with the rest of the cars around her exiting the airport. I assumed she was unaware I was behind her, or that I'd witnessed what she'd done.

I wasn't even sure who to call, and was unarmed. I couldn't say the same for Collins. Wherever she was going, I would have a hard time confronting her knowing she wouldn't be afraid to pull the trigger.

I looked at the gas gauge. There was less than a quarter-tank of gas. I hoped she wouldn't be going too far, or I'd be in trouble.

I dialed the Miami Lakes Police, and a woman answered on the second ring.

"I need to talk to Officer Cardwell," I said, my eyes on the road, watching Mia Collins take a turn.

The woman asked me to hold, but came back on the line not even thirty seconds later. "I'm sorry, Officer Cardwell is not available. I can take a message, or put you through to his voicemail?"

"Uh, voicemail's good," I said. "Thank you."

I waited, and it felt like a good minute before the phone finally rang, and picked up right away:

This is Officer Robert Cardwell with the Miami Lakes Police. Please leave a message at the tone, or press zero to be redirected back to the operator.

I decided not to leave a message, knowing the chances were slim he'd get it in time.

I followed Collins and took a turn, seeing the sign for Okeechobee Road. I hit the zero on the phone and the phone rang on the other end.

After the third ring the same woman I'd just spoken to answered. "Miami Lakes Police."

"Hi, I just called two seconds ago for Officer Cardwell. But this is an emergency," I said. "He knows who I am... I need to talk to him. I need his help."

I recognized the area Mia was heading for, and at that point knew Mia Collins was going to Helms' house.

The woman on the phone said. "Would you like to speak with another officer?"

"No! I need you to call him, have him call me," I said, trying to remember Detective Helms' address, then reciting it to the woman. "Tell him I'm on my way there now, and we're following a detective who just killed a... She killed another detective, Detective Helms, from the Miami-Dade Police."

"Sir?" she said. "This is the Miami Lakes Police Department, we're not—"

"I know what it is," I said. "But didn't you hear me? A man's been shot. An officer. Can you give me Officer Cardwell's cell number?"

"I'm sorry, sir, I'm going to hang up and contact Miami-Dade. Where did you say you were?"

"At the airport. The rooftop of the parking garage. But that's not what I'm calling about. I told you, I need Officer Cardwell's help. If you can please call him, tell him it's Henry Walsh. I'm a private investigator." I gave her Helms' address. "Tell him it has to do with what happened at the church. And the murders. He'll know what it's about."

Chapter 33

I PARKED A FEW houses down from Detective Helm's home, where Detective Collins had sat in her car with it running for a good five minutes before finally stepping out. I watched her through the trees.

She stood outside her car, looking around, as if she knew I was out there, holding her gaze almost in my direction.

Hiding behind a tree, I didn't think she could see me. But maybe I was wrong.

She walked around the side of the house, toward the back.

I started running through the wooded area, and slowed once I got to the driveway where Collins had parked her car. I looked inside at a gun left on the front seat and paused, thinking about taking it at first. But if it was the gun she used to kill Helms, and maybe the others, I wasn't about to have my fingerprints all over it.

I left the gun where it was and continued after the detective, stopping along the side of the house where I might be able to get a look at what she was doing. I heard banging, then poked my head out to see what it was.

Detective Collins had her back to me, yanking on a set of doors on a shed, shaking them frantically as if she had no way to get them open.

She said something under her breath, almost a growl, shaking the doors in apparent frustration.

The banging continued, until she stopped and turned.

I pulled my head back behind the house so she couldn't see me, waited another moment, then peered around the corner again.

She lifted a boulder from the ground and raised it over her head, smashing it against the padlocks on the shed's doors. But it didn't open, and she threw the boulder down with a scream. She shook the doors again, gasping, until she fell to her knees and cried.

I hoped the gun on the front seat was the only one she carried. But I didn't think she was dumb enough to kill Helms with her own registered gun.

Without much of a plan in my head, I walked out from the side of the house and slowly made my way toward her. But I'd only taken a couple of steps closer when Collins jumped to her feet and pulled a gun from her harness. "You fool," she said, the gun pointed at me. "What are you doing here?"

I raised my hands. "I saw what you did to Helms."

She shook her head. "I didn't do anything to Helms. You have no idea what you're talking about."

"Why'd you do it?" I said. "For money? Is that why you killed them all?"

She walked from the shed toward me, the gun aimed at my chest.

"You won't get away with it," I said. "The police are on their way. It's over, Mia."

A tear came down her cheek, the gun still raised and pointed at me.

"Did this have anything to do with your husband?" I said. "Is that what this is all about?"

"Stop talking," she said, her eyes flooded. "Just shut up!"

"I know all about him. I know how much money you both must've spent trying to save him. But why did you have to kill?" I said.

She took another step toward me, and had the gun toward my face. "I don't want to have to do this," she said.

"You don't have to," I said, trying to force myself to smile. "You really don't."

More tears came down her face. "You don't understand what it's like," she said. "I'm a cop. My husband is a... He *was* a teacher. Noble careers, right? But we couldn't afford to save his life. Do you think that's how it should be?"

"No, of course not," I said. "But I don't understand why you had to kill."

"Who said I killed anyone?" she said, shaking her head as if her conscience was torn, still denying... still hoping she'd get away with what she'd done.

"I told you already. I saw you kill Helms. But I don't understand why."

I heard a vehicle out in front of the house. "That's probably them," I said, then nodded toward the shed to hopefully distract her. "So, what is it you're trying to get out of there? Is that where you and Helms stashed the money?"

She stared back at me, as if she was thinking through her next move. Collins shook her head. "It's not what you think," she said. "I didn't plan any of this to happen this way. I swear, I…"

"But you killed them?" I said, hoping she was ready to confess. "Jillian and Brock? And Jillian's ex-husband?"

She didn't respond, her eyes shifting toward the front of the house.

I heard car doors close.

I'd kept my hands raised, but lowered them, and held out my hand. "Mia. Give me the gun. You don't want a cop to turn that corner, see you pointing that thing at me."

I certainly didn't want to be caught up in the middle of some kind of shoot-out.

She turned the gun from me and fired a shot toward the edge of the house, giving me all I needed.

I launched myself at her, taking her to the ground and trying to wrestle the gun from her.

She fired another shot just as I pinned her wrist against the damp ground.

A voice from behind me yelled, "Don't move!"

I looked back at two officers I didn't recognize, both from the Miami-Dade Police Department, their guns drawn. One of the two had his two-way, calling in that shots had been fired.

"Get this man off of me!" Collins yelled, struggling to get out from under me. "He's got my gun!"

"Drop your weapon!" one of the cops yelled, rushing toward me, gun pointed at me.

I placed her gun on the ground and raised both hands. "Don't listen to her," I said. "She killed Detective Helms."

The other officer came toward me, his gun in one hand, handcuffs in the other. "Get down on the ground!"

"She's lying," I said. "She's trying to break into this shed. There's something in there. I swear, I—"

"I told you to get down on the ground!" the cop yelled.

I had no choice but to do as I was told, and got down on my stomach.

The other cop helped Detective Collins to her feet.

"Keep your hands out where I can see them," the officer said, his knee into my back now, cuffing my wrists.

"Thank you, officer," Mia Collins said. "This man is..."

"Hey!" a voice yelled.

Officer Cardwell, from the Miami Lakes Police, walked around the corner from the front of the house. He was luckily in uniform, his gun in his hand but by his side. "This is a mistake," he said, nodding toward me. "That man didn't do anything wrong. This woman, Detective Collins, shot and killed a detective in your department. The video is already out there. Someone video'd the whole thing."

I almost smiled, thinking of Alex holding up her phone.

Detective Collins started to run toward the woods.

The officer who had started to lift me off the ground after handcuffing me, took off after her.

Officer Cardwell came over to me, helping me up. He said to the other officer, "You mind if I take these off of him?"

The one Miami-Dade officer standing with us looked confused, like he wasn't sure what he was supposed to do, at least until the other officer finally walked out of the woods with Detective Collins in custody, hands cuffed behind her back.

Collins wouldn't look at me, or anyone else, her eyes toward the ground, the cop walking her past us and taking her around the corner to the front of the house.

I turned my body, showing my own handcuffed wrists. "Can we get these off?"

The Miami-Dade officer said to Officer Cardwell, "You sure about this man?"

Cardwell nodded. "I'll do it myself, if—"

"No, no, that's all right," the cop said. "I'm just trying to understand all that's going on here, that's all." He stepped over to me, took the key from his belt and removed the handcuffs. "We're going to need an official statement from you, Mr.—"

"Walsh," I said. "Henry Walsh."

I rubbed my wrists, turning to the officer. "My partner and I—my fiancée—we witnessed Detective Collins shooting Detective Gary Helms. And, although I can't share any direct evidence with you just yet, she most likely also killed a friend of mine, his girlfriend, and his girlfriend's ex-husband."

"Is this true?" he said, looking from me to Cardwell.

I said, "I'm as certain as I've ever been."

Officer Cardwell said, "She shot that poor detective right there in broad daylight at that airport."

"He's a victim," I said. "But he's not the 'poor' detective you just described. He was involved, although I can't say to what extent. I know Alex—my partner—and I heard him say something about how she, Detective Collins, should've never killed the others. He never mentioned anyone by name, but—"

"And you'd be willing to testify?" he said. "You and your... Who is the other person? Your partner?"

"She's the one at the airport right now. She shot the video I hope is all you need."

"And what's her name?" the officer said.

"Alex Jepson," I said. "We'll do whatever we can to help. I have some other names you're going to want too."

The officer had a notepad out, taking notes.

"Maybe Detective Collins will come clean," I said. "At this point, she has nothing else to lose, right?" I went over to the shed and yanked on the doors. But they didn't budge; the lock keeping them closed looked to be military-grade, if there was such a thing. "Someone want to help me get this thing open?"

Officer Cardwell was behind me. "What's in there?"

"I'm guessing a lot of cash," I said.

He pushed me aside and pulled out his gun, firing three quick shots at the lock. It busted open and dropped to the ground. Cardwell opened the doors and we looked inside at plastic storage bins inside stacked on the far wall. There was a musty smell so strong it was almost hard to breathe.

Even with the doors wide open, the light didn't seem to be enough. I looked around, lifting the cover on the first plastic bin. I looked inside and it was filled with sand. I tried to lift it, but the bin must've weighed a hundred pounds. I tipped it over, and the sand poured out as it landed on the shed's floor.

I lifted the cover on the next bin that was under it, and all that was inside was sand. I tipped it over and the sand poured out onto what I'd already dumped.

The Miami-Dade officer said, "This what you consider a hundred grand?"

I took the cover off the next bin and inside it, as with the other two, was nothing but sand. I dragged it out of the way, and under it was what looked like a small door cut out of the wooden floor. I glanced back at the two officers and knelt down, brushing away the sand and lifting the door.

Inside it were bundles wrapped in paper—the same bundles, or at least the same paper, as what Kathy had shown me at Save-More Storage. But there were only three of the bundles in the hole, all sealed and closed with multiple layers of clear packing tape. "Anyone have a knife?" I tossed the Miami-Dade officer one of the bundles, and stood, handing the other to Cardwell. "I thought there'd be more than this." I couldn't explain why there wasn't more money.

Both Cardwell and the other officer used a knife to cut open the packages, each holding up a bundle of cash.

"This doesn't look like a hundred grand," Cardwell said.

I stood, looking at what he had in his hand. "There was a lot more than this in that storage unit," I said, looking down toward the hole in the floor.

"I'm sure Collins can tell you what happened to the rest of it," I said. "There was at least a hundred or more I saw."

I couldn't really put my finger on why Helms would pull me in, looking for the cash, if he himself had it the whole time. Something didn't add up.

I looked at the packaging it was in. "Maybe this money wasn't from the same storage unit."

I felt my phone buzz in my pocket and stepped outside to see who was calling. I didn't recognize the number, but went ahead and answered: "Henry Walsh."

There was a pause on the other end.

I said, "Hello?"

"Henry?"

I knew who it was right away and glanced over my shoulder at the two officers, watching me as if wondering what I was doing. I stepped away and whispered into the phone. "Kathy? Where the—"

"I'm okay," she said. "I know you'd want to know that. I just wanted you to know... I'm sorry I wasn't honest with you. But you also need to believe me. This wasn't always the plan."

"You expect me to believe you?" I said.

She paused on the other end. "I hope you do."

I still wasn't convinced, but I knew I'd never know the whole story.

"You can tell the cops what you want," she said. "They won't find me."

"Where are you?"

She didn't answer, and by the time I looked at the screen, she'd already hung up without another word.

Chapter 34

AFTER THREE MORE DAYS in Miami helping law enforcement tie any loose ends on the case, Alex and I were back at the marina.

On the drive back, we had discussed our immediate future. It included some changes to our wedding plans, some thoughts about living in the house I grew up in, and the boat Alex and I both felt we should enjoy more again, the way we once had.

The one thing I was sure of was that what mattered most was having Alex by my side. As far as I was concerned, nothing would ever get in the way of it, and I'd do everything possible to keep it that way.

The humidity was high in Jacksonville, maybe even more than it had been in Miami. But with the sun already down, the temperature at the marina was somewhat comfortable. Of course, I could complain about it, but I told myself not to. The thing is, a lot of what I worried about never seemed to matter much in the big scheme of things. Especially not when I was right where I was supposed to be.

Billy had met us at the marina with Raz, and brought some food from the restaurant. I had music playing on the boat, something I didn't do enough of. After meeting Joe Sheldon and seeing his huge collection of records, I knew music was something I wanted more of in my life. I wasn't about to go out and start buying vinyl records, but I was going to learn to appreciate music the way I used to.

Billy sipped an iced tea. "I don't know if you want to talk about all that happened down there in Miami, but I'm still trying to understand it all."

"There's a lot they still need to unfold," I said.

"But the detective confessed, didn't she?"

"Well, for the most part, yes. But whether or not she's told the truth is another question. She's given some names, and brought down a few of those involved so far."

"Canzano?" Billy said, not one for forgetting a name.

"Yeah, but also the owner of the storage facility. It seemed there were a lot of hands grabbing for a piece of the pie, including some dirty cops—active and retired—working with Helms and Collins."

"Wow," Billy said. "Only in Miami."

I laughed. "I wouldn't say that's true, but..."

"But I don't understand why she had to kill those people."

"Well," I said. "That's the part that isn't exactly clear. She claims she didn't like the way Jillian was starting to talk, once Jillian found out Detective Collins was involved. She claimed Jillian had gotten scared, and that had put everything at risk."

Billy said, "I would think she'd consider theft, especially for an officer of the law, to be somewhat putting everything at risk, no?" He got up from his chair and walked to the edge of the dock.

Alex said, "She gets a good lawyer, I wouldn't be surprised if the jury's somewhat sympathetic to her reason for doing it all in the first place."

"So murder, because your husband was dying of cancer, is an excusable offense now?" Billy said.

"No, I'm not saying she'll get away with it," Alex said. "But all it takes is a good lawyer and a juror or two who've dealt with insurance companies not willing to pay up, or someone who's been sick and couldn't afford the treatment..."

"I still feel there was more to it," I said. "I mean, her motive. Maybe we're never going to know. A supposed good cop like that, turns out to be a complete psycho."

We all sat quiet for a couple of moments, taking in an evening by the boat that was turning out to be a pretty nice night. It was the first time I'd felt somewhat relaxed in a while.

Billy looked at me and said, "I'm almost afraid to ask, but are you concerned at all about this Canzano guy? Don't you think he's going to blame you, for bringing the whole thing down? I'm just not sure he sounds like the kind of guy who'd be willing to forgive. And if he happens to skate..."

I could feel Alex watching me. We'd discussed it enough on the ride back, and I tried to tell her not to worry. But she'd brought it up a handful of times since we'd gotten back.

I stood up from the chair and stretched, then stepped up onto my boat. "I'm not the one who told the police he was involved. That's for him and Collins to deal with. He's going to be doing some time, unless his lawyers get him off."

"You didn't answer my question," Billy said.

I leaned with my hands on the edge of the boat, looking down at him and Alex. "I'm not concerned. I'd like to think

Canzano knows the deal. The money's gone. Kathy's husband's dead. And I wouldn't be surprised she's already out of the country."

"Was there really enough money for her to disappear like that?" Billy said.

"There was at least a hundred grand in the storage unit," I said. "Then more money at Detective Helms' place, which was apparently from another job, according to Collins. But that cash was gone missing. I can't say how much of it Kathy ended up with, but I have a feeling she has plenty."

Billy was quiet. I could see he was thinking it all through, as he always did. "I guess I'm not clear how much money we're talking about. With all these people involved, there had to be more than a couple hundred grand, no?"

I guess I hadn't explained it all very well. But there were a lot of pieces still being put together. I said, "The belief is there was plenty more from the entire operation. Some I'm sure Kathy didn't even know about. I'm not even sure Collins knew how much more there was. Last I heard, the feds had uncovered a few hundred thousand in cash. They went through every single storage unit and found more. There was a smaller unit with three washing machines, each filled with cash."

"All from one appliance store?" Billy said.

I shook my head. "No, there were more stores. The whole scheme turned out to be beyond what anyone imagined."

Billy said, "And you cracked it wide open."

I laughed. "Yeah, it's called getting lucky. Or too dumb to realize what I was stumbling in to." I turned and looked at Alex. "One of these days I'll be smart enough to listen to you."

"You never give yourself enough credit," Alex said.

I looked at her, shaking my head. "You're the one who deserves all the credit. Not only for putting up with me, but being right ninety-nine percent of the time."

She laughed and rolled her eyes. "Things could have turned out worse. You know how many people would've been tempted to take Kathy up on the offer to run off with all that money?"

The thing was, there was a short time in my life I might have. I don't mean run off with Kathy. That ship had sailed. But, the money? After I left my job in Rhode Island and all the drinking I'd been doing, at one point I was bitter enough about the law and the way things fell apart that I could have easily gone in a much different direction from where I ended up.

I still wonder, if I hadn't met Alex when I had, or if I hadn't been given a chance as director of security for the Sharks baseball team, what my life would have turned out like.

"So, now what?" Billy said, standing on the dock looking up at me on the boat. "This is probably the tenth time I've heard you say you might be done with the private eye business. But for some reason, I can't seem to believe you."

I smiled. "Maybe when we get back, I'll come work behind the bar." I glanced at Alex, who sat in her chair with her eyes out somewhere else, her gaze toward the river and the glow of the moon shining over it. She wasn't ready to believe me either.

"When do you leave?" he said.

"Thursday," I said, looking around the boat. We'd already loaded it up with whatever we thought we'd need for the trip, which wasn't much. Raz was in his bed on the boat's deck, chin on his paws, his favorite toy next to him as he looked up at me. "You ready for this, Raz?"

He lifted his head, but eased it back down.

"When was the last time you even took the boat out?" Billy said. "You sure you know what you're doing?" He laughed.

I shook my head. "No, I'm not sure. It's been a year, I'd say. Maybe even a couple of summers ago."

"And you still don't know where you're going?" he said. He looked from me to Alex.

"I'm not sure it matters," I said.

Alex smiled at me. "We'll figure it out. We always do."

· · • · • · · · ·

Ready for another mystery adventure? Jump back in time with Jake Horn, Private Investigator, to 1978 Boston, Massachusetts. *Murder at Morrissey Motel* is the first of two books in the newest series by Gregory Payette. Learn more by visiting GregoryPayette.com.

Sign up for the newsletter on my website:

GregoryPayette.com

Once or twice a month I'll send you updates and news. Plus, you'll be the first to hear about new releases with special prices. If you'd like to receive the Henry Walsh prequel (for free) use the sign-up form here:

https://www.gregorypayette.com/pages/freecrossroad

Books by Gregory Payette

For the full catalog of books, please visit GregoryPayette.com

HENRY WALSH MYSTERIES
Dead at Third
The Last Ride
The Crystal Pelican
The Night the Music Died
Dead Men Don't Smile
Dead in the Creek
Dropped Dead
Dead Luck
A Shot in the Dark
Dead or a Lie

JOE SHELDON SERIES
Play It Cool
Play It Again
Play It Down

U.S. MARSHAL CHARLIE HARLOW
Shake the Trees
Trackdown

JAKE HORN MYSTERIES
Murder at Morrissey Motel
Body on the Beach

STANDALONES/Crime
Biscayne Boogie
Tell Them I'm Dead
Drag the Man Down
Half Cocked
Danny Womack's .38

www.ingramcontent.com/pod-product-compliance
Lightning Source LLC
Chambersburg PA
CBHW061232310726
48971CB00007B/2024